CW00486924

STEP
BROTHER
bad boy

STEP
BROTHER
bad boy

VERONICA DAYE

Published by
Flirt Publishing
A Division of Jaded Speck Publishing LLC
5042 Wilshire Blvd #30861
Los Angeles, CA 90036

Stepbrother Bad Boy
Copyright © 2015 by Veronica Daye
Cover by CT Cover Designs

ISBN 978-1-939918-06-2

This book is a work of fiction. The names, characters, places, and incidents are products of the writer's imagination or have been used fictitiously and are not to be construed as real. Any resemblance to persons, living or dead, actual events, locales or organizations is entirely coincidental.

All rights reserved. No part of this book may be reproduced, scanned, or distributed in any manner whatsoever without written permission from the author except in the case of brief quotation embodied in critical articles and reviews.

Dedication

To S,
who inspires me every day.

PART I

The Devil You Know

~ One ~

"Rosalie! Hey Rosalie DeLeo!"

I looked around the open door of my locker and down the wide hall as I heard my name. Noelle, my best friend, held her books tightly to her chest as she quickly walked over with a huge smile on her face. Noelle had thick red curls, freckles, and always smelled like the bubble gum she constantly chewed.

"Did you see him today?" she asked.

"Him?"

"You know, *him*," she said, her eyes widening.

I knew who she meant, but sometimes I liked to pretend I didn't. The last thing I wanted to do was admit to anyone that he was always on my mind. Noelle leaned against the lockers while I grabbed my books for the next class.

"Yeah, I saw him after homeroom this morning. Why?" I asked.

"Because he looks so freaking hot today," Noelle said as she fanned herself. "I think I saw a new tattoo too."

He was Shane Ventana. He started at our high school last year and everyone thought he was hot. Shane had shaggy dark blond hair that fell onto his forehead and piercing green eyes. He was tattooed, mysterious, an honor roll student, and captain of the basketball team. Shane was everything rolled into one and there was no one else like him. And like most everyone else in school, Shane had no idea I was alive.

"He's been working on that sleeve for a while," I said. "My parents would kill me if I got a tattoo. I mean he's not eighteen yet, doesn't he need their permission?"

"Really? That's what you're thinking about? No wonder you're still a virgin. His tattoos make me wonder if he has any we *can't* see," she said, snapping her gum and raising her brow at the same time. "You know what I mean?"

"Everyone knows what you mean, Noelle. And I am not a virgin. You know that."

"I know you dated Ben Miller for a while, I know you had sex with him, but I'm sure he didn't make you cum. That, in my book, makes you a virgin."

"Shut up," I said, laughing.

Looking past her, I spotted Shane coming down the hall. I cleared my throat and widened my eyes, letting Noelle know he was coming this way.

Noelle calmly leaned against the lockers as I tried to not stare at him. He was wearing a pair of dark jeans with a chain that hung from his waist and a dark blue short-sleeved t-shirt that clung to his body. As he walked past a group of guys, he lifted his muscular arm and they high-fived.

Stop staring, Rosalie. Look away now. He's not blind, he's going to see you staring. Wait...is he looking at me? What do I do?!

I couldn't take my eyes off him. He was close enough that I could see the stubble on his chin that dipped into a dimple. His green eyes were right on me, but more than on me, they saw into me.

My heart pounded so loudly that I was sure everyone could hear. But he didn't turn, he didn't look away. Heat spread over my skin and up onto my cheeks.

The way he was looking at me was like he knew what I looked like naked.

Relax, Rosalie, you're not naked. Crap, why did I have to wear this stupid shirt? Naked might've been better.

"S'up," he said with the slightest nod as he walked past.

Faints.

Surprised to find myself still standing, I quickly glanced at my locker mirror. Eye liner not smudged, light brown hair not too limp, and my ugly yellow and black shirt because I didn't get to do laundry. *Just my luck that the one time he notices me, I look like an idiot.*

"Holy shit," Noelle said. "You gotta talk to him."

"What? Nooo," I said, slamming my locker door close. "He probably thought I was someone else."

"We have to go to the game tonight. Maybe he'll talk to you again."

"Tonight? I can't. I told my dad I'd go to dinner with him and Joanna."

"Your stepmom?"

"Yes, well no, they're not married. I don't think my dad will ever get married again," I said. "They've just been together forever."

The warning bell rang and Noelle and I headed in different directions to our classes. Once she was out of sight, I ran down the steps to peek out the glass doors towards the smoking porch where I knew Shane would be.

I was running out of time before class started, but I didn't care. I had to see him again. I couldn't believe he spoke to me. I didn't care that it was barely a word, it was something. He knew I existed.

Shane was sitting on one of the cement ledges that surrounded the porch. His cigarette hung from his lips. He cupped his hands around his lighter to keep it from blowing out as he lit the cigarette.

If Noelle knew I was there she would push me to talk to him, but I couldn't. I just wanted one last glimpse of him before my last class and the weekend started. As he blew the smoke from his lungs, a few cheerleaders gathered around him. He leaned towards a tall redhead next to him and kissed her. Shane didn't have one girlfriend, he had many. And I hated every one of them. Okay, maybe hate was a strong word, but I definitely envied them.

There was no way he meant to say hi to me. I was invisible in school. I was the girl without the designer clothes and with the double-digit size. I wasn't the girl that Shane Ventana noticed.

But apparently I'm the girl who stalks him, I thought.

As I headed back up the steps to the classrooms, I promised myself I would stop obsessing about him. But even as I swore it, I knew it was impossible.

~ *Two* ~

As soon as my dad honked the horn, I ran out of my bedroom and down the steps to the front door. I never liked being at home and it seemed the older I got, the more my mother and stepfather did things to make me uncomfortable. Especially my stepfather.

My parents divorced when I was five. My father was heartbroken and would give me poems and music to give to my mother, but she wanted nothing to do with him. She had already found someone else and he moved in soon after and later became my stepfather Jim. All of it left me confused.

I loved my dad and remembered doing so many things with him when I was little. But after they divorced, I hardly saw him. He wasn't allowed to call and my mother said so many bad things about him, I didn't know what to believe. It wasn't until the past year that my dad and I started spending a little more time together, but it still wasn't much.

"Where are you going?" Jim barked as I reached for the door.

"Dinner with my dad."

"You don't go anywhere without my permission."

"I told Mom," I said as I opened the door and waved to my dad.

"She should have said something to me."

Then take it up with her, I thought. I wished I could say something like that, but I didn't dare.

"I'll see you later," I said as I stepped out the door.

"Where's my kiss?"

I hate this.

I stepped back into the house and he stooped down. I quickly kissed his cheek, making sure my lips barely touched his rough skin.

"That didn't count," he said. "Do it again."

Swallowing hard, I pursed my lips again and kissed his cheek quickly, making sure my lips touched his skin even if it was only for a second. I held my breath as I waited for his verdict.

"Better," he said. "Since you're just going out for dinner, I'll expect you home in two hours."

"But I'm going out with my dad," I said.

"Two hours is enough time for dinner no matter who you're with."

I closed the door behind me and sucked in some of the cold night air. My body was in knots like it always was after talking to Jim. As I got into my dad's car, he nodded his head towards the house.

"Everything okay?" Dad asked.

Looking towards the house, I saw Jim standing in the doorway. The porch light reflected against his bald head and I imagined smashing a two-by-four into it. As I smiled at the thought, I turned back to my dad.

"Everything's fine," I said as I waved in Jim's direction.

The further Dad drove down the street, the more relaxed I felt. The knots in my body loosened up and I breathed easier.

"Where is Joanna?" I asked. "I thought the three of us were going out to dinner."

"It's going to be four of us. She had to drive to her ex's to pick up her son. They'll be meeting us at the restaurant."

"Son? I had no idea she had kids. How old is he?"

"I don't know. I think he's around your age. She doesn't talk much about him. He lives with his father."

"That's a little weird," I said.

"It was a weird situation. You probably don't remember my friend Ryan from when you were little, do you?" he asked. "This was after your mother and I..."

Got divorced. He could never say the words.

I thought for a while, trying to remember any of my father's friends, but no one came to mind. My memories were a crap shoot. Some things were as clear as if they happened yesterday while other memories just weren't there.

"No, I don't remember him."

"Ryan and I taught at the middle school together. We were really good friends, but then something happened to him. He would vanish for days and his wife, Joanna, would call me crying on the phone asking if I had heard from him. Ends up he was doing drugs.

Eventually he chose his addiction over her and they got divorced. She was really upset about it. So I guess that gave us something else in common."

"But how did Ryan get custody if he was an addict?"

He shrugged. "I don't know. It's none of my business."

They seated my father and me right away when we got to the restaurant. I sat across from my dad, assuming Joanna would want to sit next to him. My father kept checking his watch and after fifteen minutes, he started to look worried. As he stretched his neck to look towards the hostess stand, a smile spread across his face and he stood up and waved to Joanna.

I carefully folded my napkin and looked towards the doorway. Shane entered the room and slowly walked in our direction followed by Joanna. My heart leaped in my chest like a cartoon character's.

Shane's her son??

Joanna kissed my father's cheek and smiled sweetly at me. She looked perfect, like she always did. Her thick dark hair was pinned into an updo, bringing more attention to her high cheekbones and tanned skin.

As she sat down, her expertly manicured hands hung her expensive bag on the back of her seat.

Shane yanked the chair next to me out from the table and sat down. He didn't say anything, he didn't even look at the table. Other than his chair being near, he might as well have been somewhere else.

"I'm glad you could join us, Rosalie. It's always nice to see you," Joanna said.

"It's good seeing you too," I said.

I meant that. I liked Joanna. She never had a bad thing to say and she seemed to make my father happy.

"Rosalie, this is my son Shane," she said, then paused as she waited for him to reply. A brief look of disgust crossed her features. "Shane! Don't do this to me," she snapped.

I jumped at Joanna's tone, but it seemed I was the only one at the table not used to hearing it. Despite knowing Joanna for years, I suddenly felt like I didn't know anything about her at all.

Shane stretched his legs out and leaned back. He rubbed his cheek as he scanned the restaurant. I had been waiting for him to turn towards me and notice me so that I could say hi, but it was clear he could care less.

Joanna closed her eyes for a second and let out a long breath. When she opened them, a calm smile appeared on her face.

"Rosalie, I hope your father didn't spoil the surprise, but the reason we asked for you both to be here is to tell you we got married."

"We have been talking about it for a while but didn't want to make a big deal out of it since we've both been married before," Dad said. "You know I hate weddings. So we just went down to City Hall and made it official."

My crush is now my stepbrother? I have the worst luck.

I drank a sip of water and choked. As I coughed uncontrollably, Shane whacked me on the back. This wasn't the kind of attention I wanted from him. I must have done something really bad in another life.

"You couldn't tell me that over the phone?" Shane sneered at Joanna. "You made me miss the game tonight." He pulled out his cell phone and looked at the time. "I've got better places to be."

As he stood, he tapped his phone and held it up to his ear. Joanna's hand reached out and grabbed his arm, but he yanked it away and started walking to the door. With a look of sadness mixed with embarrassment, she ran after him.

"Congratulations, Dad," I said, trying to act like nothing weird happened.

"I'm sure you're surprised. You know Joanna and I have been together for years now. I thought it would be nice if you and Shane were our witnesses, but Joanna didn't want to wait." He looked towards the entrance and frowned. "Sorry about how he acted. I've only met him a few times, but Joanna tells me he gets into a lot of trouble."

"What kind of trouble?" I asked, wanting to hear more about Shane.

"I don't know the details. I'm sure it's just your typical bad boy thing. He's got the look and the attitude down. I see boys like that all the time in my school."

That look like Shane? I must be in the wrong school.

Joanna returned to the table alone with a fake smile plastered on her face. As she maneuvered into her chair, she waved off my father when he pulled the seat out for her.

"I'm sorry about that," she said. "Shane's friend picked him up, but he'll be joining us on Sunday."

"What's Sunday?" I asked.

"Sorry, I forgot to mention it to you earlier," Dad said. "We're putting an offer in on a house. We were hoping you and Shane would come and tell us what you think of it. Can you make it?"

I nodded my response, but the only thing I could think about was seeing Shane again in a couple of days.

~ Three ~

I spent most of Sunday morning trying on different outfits and discovering I hated my clothes. I needed something perfect for when I saw Shane. I didn't care how ridiculous it was, or that our parents got married, all I could think about was spending some time with Shane Ventana outside of school.

After trying on everything in my closet twice, I finally settled on a pair of jeans that made my ass look good and a blue sweater. I thought about the other girls at school who looked so put together no matter what they wore. I was sometimes jealous of them and thinking about how Shane had dated most of them, now was one of those times. I was nothing like them.

As I ran a comb through my hair one last time, my phone rang. It was Noelle. I stared at her name on the display for a moment, debating whether I should answer or not, before tapping the button.

"Hey, Noelle," I said.

"Hey, I haven't heard from you all weekend. Do you want to come over?"

Dammit! This was why I shouldn't have answered.

"I can't, my dad should be here any minute. He and Joanna are going to buy a house and they want us to see it."

"Us?" she asked.

Crap! I cannot keep a secret!

"Umm yeah, us. Joanna has a son."

"No way! You had juicy gossip like this and you didn't share?"

"Well, it's really not a big deal."

"Okay, Rosalie. Except I know you and when you say that, that means that it is. So spill."

"Fine, jeez, you can be such a bitch sometimes," I joked. "My dad and Joanna got married and now they're buying a house together. That's it."

"Hmm, you're leaving something out," she said. "Tell me about Joanna's son. They've been together a while so he's not a baby. Is he hot? Is that why you've been quiet?"

Fuck! How do I get out of this? I can't lie to her.

As my mind whirred, my dad's silver Toyota pulled up in front of the house. While I couldn't lie to Noelle, I could easily delay telling her the truth.

"I'll call you later," I said. "Dad just got here."

"Don't hang up," she said. "You gotta tell me!"

I ended the call and slipped the phone into my pocket as I ran down the stairs. Glancing towards the living room, I was glad to not find anyone there. My mother knew I was going out with Dad and that was all that mattered to me. I didn't want to deal with Jim.

As I opened the car door, I realized only two people were in the car, my dad and Joanna. My heart sank a little as I slid into the back seat.

"That sweater looks very pretty on you," Joanna said as I buckled my seatbelt.

"Thanks. So where's the house?"

"It's just up here," Dad said as he turned the corner.

"Seriously?"

"It's a nice neighborhood, and I was hoping if I lived closer we could see each other more," he said.

He pulled up in front of a white split-level house. A woman with short blonde hair in a suit was standing in the house, on the other side of the clear storm door. She opened the door, then smiled and waved as we walked up the driveway.

"I don't want to get in your way so I'll be in my car," she said. "Please take your time looking around. I know this is a big decision."

As we walked through the house, my dad explained all the things he planned to do. I half-listened to something about replacing the tiles in the bathroom and the cabinets in the kitchen, but I couldn't focus on anything he said. All I wanted to know was where Shane was.

"Come on," Joanna said. "I'll show you the bedrooms."

I followed her up the steps and she stopped at the first door on the left.

"This is your room," Dad said. "It even has its own bathroom."

"*My* room?"

"In case you want to move in or just spend the night," he said. "You know I've always kept a room for you."

I stepped into the light-filled room with wood floors and looked back at them. I didn't know what to say or even if I should say something. Living with my father was never something that crossed my mind.

"Thanks, but--"

"So the princess gets a room? What about me?" Shane's deep voice echoed in the empty house. My heart leapt as he appeared in the doorway.

"I didn't think you were coming," Joanna said. "There's a room for you too. If you want it."

Joanna's heels clicked loudly on the wood floor as she walked down the hall to the next bedroom. Shane didn't follow her. He stood in the hall, his hands deep in his pockets.

His eyes narrowed as he looked towards his mother standing outside the doorway of the next room.

"Be honest, Mom," he said. "You're happier when I'm not around."

Shane turned and even though I couldn't see him, I heard the thud of his boots disappearing down the stairs. A few seconds later, the storm door slammed and I jumped.

As Dad and I stepped into the hall, Joanna wiped a tear away then disappeared into a bedroom across the hall. My dad went after her. Without thinking about it, I went down the steps after Shane.

Shane was pacing the driveway while he smoked. He didn't look up as I walked towards him. I wasn't sure he knew I was there or if he just wanted to be alone so he was ignoring me, but something about him drew me in.

"Are you alright?" I asked.

"Did she send you out here? No, wait, let me guess, she didn't."

"Listen, I don't understand why you're being like this. I've seen you at school and--"

"And what? I shouldn't act like this? You think you know all about me because you've seen me at school? You don't know shit about me. You don't even remember me, do you?"

Remember you? You're all I can think about.

I didn't have the nerve to say what I was thinking. I just stood there, confused with how he was talking to me. I took a deep breath to calm myself before I said something stupid while he took another drag of his cigarette.

"You have no fucking clue what I'm talking about, do you?" he asked, his voice a growl.

"Of course I remember you. You just said hi to me the other day. You started school with us last year."

He scoffed as he tossed the cigarette to the ground and crushed it with his boot.

"I'm not surprised. My own mother barely remembers me. I'm sure she wasn't thrilled when Dad and I moved back to town."

Shane tilted his head as he stepped closer to me. His green eyes flicked behind me towards the house.

"I'll see you tomorrow," he said. "Try not to be so obvious when you're spying on me."

My eyes widened and my cheeks began to burn as he walked away. All this time I thought I had been smart, I thought I was invisible to him and that he never saw me. Now I wondered how long it had been since he first caught me.

As he got into his car, I wanted to say something. I had to defend myself and make up some excuse to prove him wrong, but my feet were cemented to the driveway.

~ *Four* ~

Noelle backed her green Chevy coupe out of the driveway as I pulled my make-up out of my bag. It didn't matter how early I got up in the morning, I could never seem to be on time for when Noelle picked me up for school.

"I should be angry at you for not calling me back yesterday," Noelle said.

"You could never be angry with me, you love me, remember?" I grinned at her as I brushed some color on my cheeks. "Is my blush even?"

"No, a little too much on the left. Seriously, Rosalie, I've been dying to know what happened. If my cousins didn't come over yesterday I would've kept bugging you until you gave in."

"I know, I know," I said. "I'm sorry. I think I was just a little weirded out by what happened. So you know I went out to dinner with my dad and Joanna on Friday. Well, Joanna and her son met us there, and Shane is her son."

"Get out! No freaking way. Shane, like our Shane, like the guy you stalk Shane?"

"The one and only."

"Fuck. Wait, you said they got married? So that means Shane is your *brother*? Holy shit!"

"Exactly! Now you get why I was so weirded out. Of all the dumb luck, right?"

"So that means I can date him, right? I mean, you can't, so there's nothing that says I can't now. You know, like friend code or something."

"You bitch," I said, laughing. "No, the friend code still applies, I still like him so you can't date him. It's not like we grew up together. He just became my stepbrother."

"Whatever, you're gross."

She laughed as she pulled into the school parking lot and drove slowly as she looked for Shane's wreck of a car. It was something we got into the habit of doing every morning.

Noelle and I went our own ways to drop our things off in our lockers. As I shoved my backpack away, Seth DeMarco opened his locker next to mine.

Seth and I had been in the same homeroom for years because our last names started the same. Some of the kids used to make fun of him because he was overweight and wore thick glasses, but I always thought he was a nice guy and someone I considered a friend.

"Hey, Rosalie," Seth said. "Can you do me a favor?"

Seth looked at the floor, then down the hall towards the doorway. I turned around to see if he was looking at anyone, but no one else was around.

"Sure, what is it?" I asked.

"It's nothing really. I'm not going to be in homeroom and I can't get back to my locker later so I was wondering if you could do me a favor. Can you hold onto my eyeglass case for me?"

Seth reached up to the top shelf of his locker and pulled out a large, hard eyeglass case. As he held it in his hands, I couldn't help but be reminded of a coffin in a Star Trek movie I watched with my dad on television years ago.

"Yeah, no problem," I said. "Do you want to meet somewhere so I can get it back to you?"

"Don't worry about it, I'll find you when I need it." Seth pushed his wire rim glasses up his nose, then looked back down the hall towards the doorway to the cafeteria. "Thanks for doing this for me. Oh, and one more thing. Don't open it."

I held the eyeglass case as he hurried away. I looked at it again and thought it felt a little heavy for an empty case, but then shoved it onto the top shelf in my own locker. The warning bell rang and I slammed my locker door shut and rushed to get to homeroom on time.

***

Two periods had passed and I couldn't stop thinking about Seth's eyeglass case in my locker. *Why shouldn't I open it?* If he hadn't said to not open it, I wouldn't have given it any thought.

I had study hall third period and went back to my locker to drop off my books. The eyeglass case was sitting there, staring at me, mocking me, begging for me to open it. I couldn't take it any more. Maybe Seth was just testing me, but I had to open it.

I waited until the bell rang and then made sure I was the only one in the hall. As I pulled the case down, it felt even heavier than before. *There has to be something in here, but what? Another pair of glasses?*

The black case creaked as I slowly opened it. The stench of tobacco hit my nostrils, making me scrunch my face. In a baggie was enough tobacco to fill the entire case. I thought about my grandfather who smoked a pipe, but it didn't make any sense. Why would Seth have tobacco?

I closed the case, slid it to the back of the top shelf, and closed my locker. Leaning against it, I saw Shane walk past the cafeteria doorway and before I could talk some sense into myself, I went after him hoping he could help.

"Shane! Wait up," I called out.

He turned towards me, his face a mixture of disgust and confusion.

"Is this how it's going to be? Now that you're my *sister* you think I'm going to talk to you? Or maybe you want to join the Shane club. I bet you still have your 'V' card, and that's the price of admission. You're not my usual type, so I'll think of you as community service."

"I...uhh..." I couldn't get any words out. I didn't expect him to act like such an ass. *Why did he hate me?* "Never mind," I said.

As I spun on my heel to get away from him, I heard him mutter something before reaching out to grab my arm.

"What do you want?" he demanded.

As he glared at me, I wanted nothing more than to forget I ever had a crush on him. But even with the mixed feelings going on in my head, my body was responding to him touching my arm. Something had to be wrong with me.

"I said never mind. You obviously don't want to help me and I don't even know if I need help. I was confused and I saw you and thought maybe you could help me. I didn't realize you were such a fucking asshole," I said.

"Why are you talking so much?"

"I don't know why. You're being an ass and I'm confused. Whenever I get nervous, I start babbling and I can't stop. I don't know what it is, but I can't help it."

Shane's hands reached for my face and pulled me close. His lips pressed against mine and all my nervousness melted away. As his tongue moved hungrily into my mouth, his fingers wrapped around my hair, keeping me close.

He pulled away with a jerk and his intense green eyes bored into me.

His kiss left me breathless and dizzy. His lips moved, but I couldn't hear the words, all I could do was wish they were back against mine. Forcing my brain to take over made me realize how much of an effect Shane had on my body. And as I looked at the glint in his eyes, I knew he knew it too.

Keep it together, Rosalie. Don't act like such a loser, it was just a kiss.

"What was that for?" I croaked.

"I had to shut you up somehow. Figured maybe if your panties were wet you wouldn't be so nervous."

"You're such an ass. I liked you better when I didn't know you."

"Whatever. You came after me, remember? What do you want?"

"A friend of mine gave me something to hold and told me to not open it," I said.

"So you opened it, didn't you?"

"Of course I did, wouldn't you?"

"Go on, I don't have all day. Who was this friend?"

"You probably don't know him. He's in my homeroom and his locker is right next to mine. He gave me his eyeglass case and said he'd get it from me later."

"Jeez, Rosalie, I didn't ask for the long version, just gimme a name."

"Seth DeMarco."

"Seth? Fat fuck with glasses?"

"Yeah, he's overweight, but--"

"What, are you into him? Are you dating that needledick?"

"No, we're just friends and he gave me--"

"Where is it?"

"In my locker. But I don't think it's a big deal. It's just his eyeglass case."

"Shh. You talk too much."

Shane grabbed my arm again and led me towards my locker. When we got there, he looked around and then yanked on the dangling combination lock.

"Open it," he grumbled.

My fingers trembled as I turned the dial. I was still having a hard time concentrating. All I could think about was his kiss, the warmth of his lips, how demanding his tongue was.

I opened my locker and pulled down Seth's case. Shane took it, looked around quickly, then motioned for me to step closer. He must have known what to expect and was shielding the contents in case someone walked past. As he opened it, the strong tobacco scent sprung forward.

"Holy *shit!* I knew he was dealing," Shane said.

"Dealing? Who buys tobacco? I thought kids bought cigarettes all the time without any problem. Why would they want loose tobacco?"

"Are you for real? Are you that naive?" Shane's eyes squinted and his brow wrinkled as he searched my face. He shook his head slightly. "No wonder you're the princess. Princess Rosalie. What kind of name is that anyway? Rosalie. It suits you though, you're out of touch just like an old lady."

I swiped the case from his hands and slammed it shut. He didn't need to tell me it wasn't tobacco. Just from his reaction to me, I knew it was pot.

"Well excuse me for not recognizing drugs when I see them," I said. "And I love my name. I was named after my grandmother and I have a lot of memories of her. My name makes me feel closer to her. Not that you'd care about any of that."

With the case in my hands, I walked towards the garbage can at the entrance of the cafeteria. Shane's boots thudded behind me until I felt his hand on my shoulder.

"I'm sorry," he said.

I turned to face him, ready to give him hell, but the expression on his face told me he was sincere.

"I know what it's like to be close to your grandmother. And to miss her," he said quietly.

"Fine, whatever. Let's just forget about it."

With his head hanging down, he nodded. I waited for him to meet my gaze, but he wouldn't look at me. Hearing him mention his own grandmother made me realize how little we knew about each other even though we were now technically related.

Glancing up at the clock, I saw the period was almost over. I had to get rid of the pot. Seth gave it to me for a reason and there was no way I was taking the fall for it. It could ruin my chances for getting into college.

Shane grabbed my arm as I started walking back towards the cafeteria.

"Where do you think you're going with that?" he asked.

"The garbage. I'm throwing it away."

"Are you crazy? You can't just throw away that much pot."

"Why? Because you want to smoke it?"

"No, because someone will find it. I bet Seth heard they're doing a search today. That's why he gave it to you, he didn't want to get caught."

"Then what do I do with it? Should I take it to the office?"

"No, they'll never believe you. And you want to go to college, right? You're never getting in with a record. Give it to me. I'll take care of it."

As he took the case from me, the bell sounded and the hall filled with people. One of Shane's friends, Warren, walked past and held his hand up to high-five Shane.

"New addition to the club?" Warren asked as he nodded in my direction.

"Nah man, she's no one," Shane said.

She's no one. Ouch!

I was always a no one, but it never hurt or bothered me as much as when I heard Shane say it. I went through the rest of the day in a daze, thinking about his kiss and how he helped me, but that wasn't all of it, there was the other side of him that was a jerk to me. Sometimes I wanted to hate him just because he seemed to hate me so much, too.

I avoided my usual routes to class. I didn't want to see him, not after he said I was no one. A crowd had gathered in the glass entryway near the stairway to my classes. Noelle was towards the back of the crowd, away from the glass doors, texting.

"What's going on?" I asked.

"There you are! I've been looking all over for you. Did you hear?"

"Hear what?"

A hush went through the crowd as four policemen entered the hall. Between them were Seth and Shane, handcuffed, their faces expressionless. Everything was silent except for the thud of Shane's boots. Or maybe that was my heart.

As they exited the building, the crowd moved to the glass doors, following them. I pushed my way in front of them and watched as the cops pushed Shane's head down as he got into the backseat of one of their cars. Seth was placed in the back of another police car.

Neither Shane nor Seth returned to school. Four months later, I graduated with my father and Joanna in attendance. During that time, neither of them said anything about Shane and I didn't know how to bring him up to ask. No one said anything about him, not even at school. I might as well have made him up, he didn't exist.

I spent the rest of high school following my usual pattern of looking in the halls for him. It was the least I could do to keep my memory of him around. Whatever happened to him, it happened because of me.

Shane disappeared for me. Maybe he didn't really hate me.

When I got my acceptance letter to Arizona State University, I silently thanked Shane for sacrificing himself so I didn't have to stay at home. Not that he knew anything about my home life, no one did. No one knew what I was dealing with. I had to get out of there and going away to college was the only answer.

~ Five ~

Parking my navy blue boat of a car at the curb, I looked up at my home. The tan siding and cornflower blue shutters looked welcoming, but all I felt was dread. Was this how my friends felt when they came home? I doubted it.

Since the summer began, my stepfather lost his job and was home all the time. To help support the family, I started working full time at the bank. My time at work was the only thing keeping me sane while I waited to move to school.

I hardly saw Noelle anymore. My mother and stepfather had made my going anywhere but to work so difficult that I gave up trying. Luckily she met a new guy and spent a lot of her free time with him. The times we did talk, I never mentioned what was going on at home. I couldn't. It was something I wanted to forget.

As I entered the house, Jim rushed over, towering over me. His face was stern and his eyes flashed with anger. I couldn't help it, I immediately felt guilty. I had to have done something to make him so angry, I just didn't know what it was.

"Where's the key?" he demanded.

"What key?" I asked, genuinely confused.

"The one for the lock you put on your door. You know I need access to your bedroom."

"No, you don't. I'm paying for food and utilities, I'm giving you and Mom money when you need it, I'm even paying for your credit cards. And I'm eighteen. I deserve a little privacy."

My eyes filled with tears and I ran up the stairs to my room, quickly unlocked the door, then collapsed onto the floor. I couldn't take it much longer. When he started coming into my bedroom at night, I knew I needed to do something to protect myself so I bought a lock.

On the floor next to my desk was the backpack I used to carry every day to school. I refused to put it away because it was the only thing that reminded me of the simpler times. When my only worry was whether Shane would catch me spying on him.

Shane. Just thinking about him made me feel better. In the time since I had last seen him, I built him up even more. He barely knew me, but he took the blame for the pot. At least that was the story I told myself. I doubted I would ever know the truth.

***

The next day as I was leaving for work, I heard my mother call for me from the kitchen.

"Rosalie, do you have a minute?"

I couldn't say no to her even though I was already running a little late. As I entered the kitchen, I found my mother sitting at the kitchen table stirring honey into her coffee.

"Hi Mom," I said. "I only have a minute. Is something wrong?"

"Jim spoke to me about the lock on your door. It's fine if you want to have one, but you have to give him the key."

"Why does he need a key to my bedroom?"

I swallowed hard as I waited for the question to sink into my mother's mind. It didn't phase her though.

"Jim needs access to your bedroom. What if there was an emergency?"

I stared at my mother for a minute, unable to understand how she could ignore the obvious.

"No, Mom," I whispered, shaking my head. "This isn't right."

"Jim is expecting the key by the end of the day."

I blinked back tears as I left the house and sank into the spongey driver's seat of my car. Things had been so hard the past couple of weeks at home. I was feeling raw. I was on the verge of tears constantly and the only thing keeping me going was the ticking down of the clock for college to start.

My day at work flew by and before I knew it, I was on my way home. During lunch, I went online and looked at photos of the ASU campus and imagined myself there. I couldn't wait.

Once I got home, I grabbed the mail from the mailbox and flipped through the envelopes looking for bills I needed to pay for my mother or anything with my name on it. To my surprise, there was a thin envelope from Arizona State admissions. I tore it open before entering the house.

Dear Rosalie DeLeo,

Thank you for contacting our Admissions Department with the change in your student status. As I indicated over the phone, with the school year starting soon, this decision is final. Your admission has been delayed until the next school year as requested.

Sincerely,
Scott Overmeyer
Dean of Admissions

What the FUCK?!?

I ran into the house, tears streaming down my face. I dropped the mail on the dining room table and pulled my phone out of my bag. Angrily wiping at my tears, I tried to read the phone number on the page so I could dial.

"This has to be a mistake," I muttered.

My mother stepped out of the kitchen, her face expressionless. She entered the dining room, her ever-present mug of coffee in her hand.

"Is something wrong?" she asked.

No, I like crying hysterically for the hell of it.

I couldn't answer her. And even if I could, I wouldn't be able to say what I was thinking. I handed her the letter. She looked it over and shrugged.

"I called them last week," she said. "You have new responsibilities now that Jim is out of work."

"How could you?"

I collapsed into a chair, sobbing. I was stuck, trapped in a nightmare. My chest ached.

"It was Jim's idea. He doesn't want you to go away either. He's having a hard time finding a job. I think they blackballed him at his old job. Such a shame after twenty years," she said before taking a sip of her coffee. "No one is calling him for interviews and you don't expect me to go back to work, do you? If college means that much to you, I'm sure your acceptance at Rutgers is still valid and they're only ten minutes away. You can live at home."

I'd rather die.

I couldn't speak to her anymore. I couldn't even look at her. I grabbed my things and headed towards the stairs. Just beyond them, Jim was sitting in the living room watching television.

"You never left the key to your room," he said.

There was no point in answering. I knew I'd pay for it later, but I ignored him and climbed the stairs. I just wanted to be alone in my room and cry.

As I got to the landing, I knew something wasn't right. The hall had a lot more light than it usually did. My pace quickened as I walked down the hall and then I saw what was wrong.

My bedroom door had been taken off of its hinges. I felt like the air had been sucked out of me. Like the door leaning against the wall had been slammed into my body.

I needed to be alone. I needed to have some space to just lock the door and not worry about someone coming in. Flicking on the bathroom light, I slammed the door shut and reached for the knob to lock it. The lock was gone.

"This isn't right, this just isn't right," I whispered.

My tears had dried up. I felt nothing but emptiness. I was numb. I needed to figure out how to survive here until I could move out.

I entered my room and slid the door so it covered most of the doorway. My stomach clenched as I looked around the bedroom. Some things had been moved around from where I left them. It was another one of the reasons why I installed the lock. I was tired of feeling violated in the place I should feel the most secure and safe.

Settle down, Rosalie.

Taking a deep breath, I sat on my daybed in the corner of the room. I tried to calm myself like I always needed to whenever my stepfather had been in my room. I set my bag down next to me on the bed and placed my hand over my stomach, hoping to calm it with deep breaths.

It didn't work. As I sat there, I noticed my underwear drawer was slightly open. Underwear was the one thing I splurged on, and seeing my drawer like that reminded me of my favorite panties.

They had gone missing about a month ago. They were dark purple satin with black lace along the hips and they cost way too much for something no one but me would see, but I had to have them. I always did my own laundry so I knew they didn't got lost in a hamper. There was only one place they could be.

Perverted sonofabitch!

Getting up from the bed, I stood in front of my dresser as I wondered which pair was missing this time. Holding my breath, I opened the drawer. Lying on top were my favorite undies. They had magically been returned. They were lying flat on top of everything. There was no way I could have missed them.

That was the last straw. I grabbed the panties as I heard my mother walking down the hall. In her arms were several shopping bags with Macy's on them.

I held up the panties as I tried to rein in my anger. "Did you do this?" I asked. "Did you put them back in my drawer?"

"Oh, is that the pair you lost?"

Without looking at me, she turned into her bedroom. I followed her. I couldn't just ignore it anymore. I was done keeping my mouth shut about her husband and the things he did in my bedroom.

"You know I didn't lose them," I said. "Was it you? Or did he put them back? I can't help but notice they magically returned two days after I told you they were missing and the same day my door was taken off its hinges."

"I'm sure they've been in your drawer all this time. You've never been very observant."

Clenching my fists, I had to control the urge to hit something. I wasn't a violent person, but at that moment everything came together and I was done.

"I'm done with this, Mom. I've had enough. I can't live like this anymore."

"What are you talking about now?" she said with a sigh.

"I have no privacy. I can't go out with friends. I can't talk on the phone without him listening in. These are the things I'm talking about. Things that you know about. I can't even have a lock on the door to my room."

"You know the reason for that. Jim said he needs access to every bedroom at all times of the day or night. What if there was a fire?"

I knew fire was a big thing with my mother. When she was a kid, the apartment building they lived in caught fire. They didn't have much, but they lost everything. I already knew about Jim needing access to my bedroom at all times. I felt sick thinking about it and how my mother always turned a deaf ear and a blind eye to it.

"I'm moving out," I said.

She laughed. "Where do you think you're going?"

I didn't have many options. Maybe I could rent a room. I knew at this point I wouldn't be able to get a dorm at Rutgers. That was even assuming I could go there. I wasn't even sure how I would afford a place and still go to school, but I knew I couldn't live with my mother and stepfather anymore. There was only one option left.

"I'll move in with Dad," I said.

She laughed and began pulling her new clothes out from the bags. Holding up a little black dress against her body, she turned to me. "What do you think? Nice? It was on sale," she said.

"Did you hear me?"

"What? That joke about living with your dad? Yes, I heard that. You go right ahead. You think we're strict, just wait until you see how your dad is."

That was the problem. I didn't know my dad that well. With him and Joanna living around the corner, I saw him a little more frequently, but we never spoke very much. I always felt like we were both still trying to get to know each other.

Whenever I went to his house, Dad reminded me I had a bedroom. Joanna had decorated it with photos of my dad and I through the years and the room always had fresh flowers in it. But it felt like a shrine, not my bedroom.

My mother was right. I didn't really know what it would be like living with him. I hadn't spent more than a day with my father in thirteen years. As Mom continued looking over her new clothing, I heard Jim's footsteps on the stairs. I had a choice to make--the devil I knew or the one I didn't.

"I'm moving in with Dad."

PART II

The Boy Next Door--Literally

~ Six ~

Living with my dad and Joanna ended up being one of the best decisions I had ever made. The only downside to the month I had been there was my obsession over what happened to Shane at school grew even more.

There weren't any photos of Shane anywhere in the house. Joanna never mentioned him either. It had been six months since I last saw him, but whenever I closed my eyes, I could still feel the heat of his lips pressed against mine.

With only a few weeks left before I started college at Rutgers, I was working part time at the bank, but now my money was going to go towards saving for school, which my father said he'd help pay for. I didn't think things could get better.

As I walked up the driveway after working that morning, Dad and Joanna were leaving the house. I smiled at Joanna, but she walked past me as if I wasn't there and got into the passenger seat of my dad's Toyota.

"Is she alright?" I asked.

"She'll be fine. She's just anxious," Dad said. "Shane is coming. We're going to pick him up now."

Shane is coming! The one guy I lusted after in high school is coming here!

"I can go with you. Where has he been?" I asked, trying to control my inner cheerleader.

"I think it's better if you stay here. Joanna's already pretty upset." My father lowered his voice. "Don't say anything, but your stepbrother was in jail again."

"*Again?*"

"I told you, he's messed up. He's had a tough life. I can't get into it now, but I'm sure you'll find out soon enough. One of the terms of his parole is that he can't live with his father because of all the trouble he's been in. I don't know how long he'll be here, but he's moving in."

I waved as my dad and Joanna drove away, but the real reason I was still outside was that I was too stunned to move. The one guy I had lusted over for the past year was going to be under the same roof, in the same house, sleeping on the other side of a wall from me.

***

It felt like forever before I heard my dad's car back in the driveway. I had changed out of my work clothes into a pair of jeans, but I barely remembered doing it. All I could think about was Shane coming and his being in jail. Again.

Again? I wanted to find out answers. Why was he there? I had a hard time believing Seth's pot was enough to put him away for so long, but what else could have happened to him? I had to know.

As soon as Shane got out of the car, I could see the difference six months away made. His shoulders looked wider and the muscles on his arms were thicker than they were before. He had sunglasses covering his eyes and his hair was shorter. His clenched jaw told me he did not want to be here.

Shane was walking ahead of them carrying a large duffel bag. I opened the door as they approached and he took a step back when he saw me. His face contorted with disgust.

"What the fuck is she doing here?" he asked.

He pushed past me, his boots echoing through the house as he headed straight for the stairs. Joanna looked worn out and my dad looked helpless as they came in. It was obvious neither of them was going to explain anything.

I felt uneasy hearing Shane's footsteps in the hall upstairs. I didn't know if he remembered which room was his, and I was still sensitive about my space. I heard my bedroom door creak open and raced after him.

"That's not your room," I said.

He looked around. "It's nice though. Maybe we should switch."

"You haven't even seen your room. It's nice too."

"I don't need to see it. I know the princess gets the better room." He took his sunglasses off and glared at me. "Right, *sis?*"

I cringed hearing him call me that. Somehow, in my excitement of hearing he was coming back, I forgot one simple thing. We were now related.

He pushed past me and walked further down the hall to his room. The door slammed shut.

I closed my bedroom door and was about to head down the stairs when I turned around and walked down the hall to his bedroom. I didn't know what his problem with me was, but if he was going to live here, I needed to talk to him. I knocked on the door.

"Go the fuck away," he said.

I raised my hand to knock again, but didn't. *What was I doing?* He obviously didn't want to talk to me, so why was I pushing?

From the first moment I saw Shane, there was something about him I couldn't resist. I was never the kind of girl to follow a guy or swoon whenever one was around. Hell, I was never the girl who used the word swoon. But that had been Shane's effect on me from day one, and it didn't change now that he was back.

As I came downstairs, I overheard my dad and Joanna talking in the kitchen. I stopped on the steps where they couldn't see me so I could listen.

"How long do you think Shane will stay?" Dad asked.

"I don't know. He's never wanted to stay with me before. Knowing him, he'll get himself in trouble again soon. I'm just worried because he's an adult now."

"I'm going to check on Rosalie."

Crap! I'm caught!

"Oh, there you are," Dad said, looking surprised. "Let's go for a walk."

That was my dad's code for when he wanted to talk to me without Joanna around. I put on my sneakers and we headed out the door. We were a block away from home before my dad spoke.

"I wanted to talk to you about Shane," he said.

"You mean your son?" I teased.

"No, please don't call him that. He's not my son." He laughed and rolled his eyes. "I just want to make sure you're okay with him living here. Joanna didn't tell me he was coming until this morning. I don't think she expected him to stay."

"You said he was in jail?"

He nodded. "Yeah, for drugs, like his dad. I don't know everything, but he's had a rough life. I really think he's a good kid, he just needs someone to believe in him."

I felt so bad hearing Shane was in jail for drugs, I couldn't say anything else. Questions swam through my head, but I knew my dad didn't have the answers. If I wanted to know what really happened, I needed to get Shane to talk to me.

"I just wanted to tell you that if you feel uncomfortable with him here, just say the word and he's gone."

"No, I'm fine," I said. "I'm sure everything will be okay."

When we got back from our walk, Joanna said dinner was almost ready. I went to my room to change clothes. I was a little sweaty and figured I could take a quick shower before dinner.

The bathroom door was closed, but sometimes I did that out of habit. I opened the door and a wall of steam enveloped me.

What the hell? Did I leave the water running?

As I entered the bathroom, the shower curtain was pulled back and Shane stepped out and onto the fuzzy rug. He was naked except for the towel he was drying his hair with.

I wanted to turn around and leave the bathroom, but I was paralyzed. The water dripping down his body was mesmerizing. And when my eyes reached his cock, I let out a small gasp. I had never seen one so big.

"Do I get a welcome fuck?" he asked.

"A what?"

"Why else would you be in here? Didn't you hear the shower?"

"I forgot we shared a bathroom."

"You can't even stop looking at it, can you?"

"I...uhh...wow," I stammered.

"Hello to your *big* brother, huh?" he said with a laugh. "You know where to find me if you ever need it. Maybe this arrangement isn't so bad. How about a little *tit* for tat?"

He flexed his muscles, making his tattoos jump, and I couldn't help but laugh.

"I promise I won't tell," he said as he cocked his brow.

He left the bathroom and I splashed water on my face, trying to get the image of his cock out of my mind, but it was firmly planted in there. Firmly. And I had to admit I didn't mind.

Dinner was almost ready so I didn't have enough time to shower. I was a little worried Shane might walk in on me for a little *tit for tat* anyway. The night was warm so I put on a pair of shorts with a t-shirt and went downstairs.

My father sat at the head of the table with Joanna on one side and an empty spot on the other. Next to the empty spot was Shane. He gave me a big smile and patted the empty seat.

"Saved a seat for you, sis."

"I'm *not* your sister," I muttered as I passed him.

I sat next to him and like a magnet, my eyes went to his lap. His jeans were so tight I could see the outline of his dick. He grabbed his bulge and I looked up and caught his sly look. I knew I was in trouble.

Throughout dinner, I forced myself to not look at Shane. I refused to look in his direction. I was on edge. What if he said something about my looking at him?

"I hope you're settling in, Shane," my dad said.

"Yeah, I think I'll have a good time here. I took a shower before and our Rosalie here--"

"I swear I didn't see anything," I blurted out.

My father gave me a weird look but didn't say anything. I looked down and my eyes went back to Shane's bulge again.

Dammit! Look away, Rosalie!

"As I was saying, our Rosalie here has a nice selection of bath wash and shampoo. I hope you don't mind that I used your stuff."

"It's no problem," I said, wishing dinner was over.

"If I have anything you want, you know where to get it," he said, grinning. "I'm a firm believer in tit for tat."

My cheeks burned, but I kept my eyes on my plate and pushed the food around. I couldn't eat, my mind was elsewhere.

I poured myself a glass of water and as I took a sip, Shane's hand touched my bare thigh. I tried to act cool, like nothing was happening, but then his hand moved up, closer to my shorts. I jerked my leg away and spilled some water onto me.

"I'm sorry I got you wet," Shane whispered. "By the way, your nipples are hard."

I folded my arms over my chest and tried to act like nothing happened. Shane stood from the table and picked up his plate.

"I love eating out in my bedroom," he said.

"That's fine, dear," Joanna said. "Let me know if you need anything."

Eating out. Part of me wanted to laugh, part of me was horrified by how immature he was acting, but another part of me desperately wished I was his dinner.

***

The next day I found Shane pacing in front of the front bay window. His hands opened and closed into fists and I could hear him muttering, but I couldn't hear what he was saying. I thought about what my father said about drugs and wondered if I was wrong about it being my fault.

"You have a car, right? You have to drive me into town," he said.

"What for? What makes you think I want to drive you anywhere?"

"Because you're a nice person and not a bitch. Although I've been wrong before."

"Tell me why you were such an asshole to me yesterday and I'll drive you."

"It's complicated," he said. "Forget I asked."

"Then at least tell me what happened that day in school with Seth."

"I'll tell you during the drive."

"Fine," I said as I grabbed my keys. "Where are we going?"

"Just drive downtown, I'll let you know when we get there."

As I started the engine, I couldn't help thinking *wow! Shane Ventana is in my car!* It made me feel like an idiot. I tried to act calm and cool, like it wasn't a big deal, but deep inside I was a nervous wreck. Any minute now I'd do something stupid like when I choked at dinner. That was my luck.

"So what happened at school?" I asked.

"I'm sure you heard. I was arrested. They sent me to juvie."

"But you didn't do anything."

"Didn't matter," he said. "I had enough priors. The judge thought he could threaten me with juvie and I'd tell them everything they wanted to know."

"Then why didn't you? Why would you protect Seth?"

"It wasn't Seth I was protecting," he said. "What happened to me wasn't about Seth's deals. They got him so they were happy. Unfortunately, my priors came up and that caused some problems."

"What did you do?"

"That's none of your business."

Shane turned towards the window and was quiet for a moment. I didn't know what to think anymore. Was it my fault he ended up in jail? Or would he have ended up there eventually anyway?

"Turn up here," he said. "Make this right."

"There? Are you crazy?"

"Just do it."

We were in a part of town I only drove through before and usually with my windows up and the doors locked. The old brick buildings were worn and several were boarded up. The turn Shane wanted me to make looked more like an alley than a street.

He's going to buy drugs, I thought.

The alley led to a small parking lot. I stopped the car and Shane got out then popped his head back into the car.

"You coming?" he asked.

"No, I think it's better if I stay right here."

"All alone in your big ass boat? I don't think your dad would like that."

He closed the car door and started walking towards a peeling white door with a faded sign I couldn't read. Shane turned back to me and grinned before disappearing inside.

The minutes dragged by slowly. Every sound made me jump. A large van entered the parking lot and parked close to my car, and every serial killer I had heard about flashed across my mind. I'd had enough of my overactive imagination and turned the car off and rushed over to the door Shane had entered.

A musty smell hit me as I entered and I fought the urge to sneeze. When I looked around, I realized I was in an art supply store. Aisles of paints, paper, canvas, pencils, everything imaginable was in front of me.

I started walking past the aisles wondering where Shane was and found him filling a basket with oil and acrylic paints.

"Why couldn't you tell me this was where you wanted to go?" I asked.

"Because I wanted to see if you trusted me enough to just take me."

"So you were testing me?"

He shrugged. "I don't trust many people, why would anyone trust me?"

"So you paint?"

"When I can. It relaxes me."

"Can I see your work?"

"No," he said gruffly. "I don't share it with anyone. And don't tell anyone you brought me here either."

"But what about--"

"I'm serious, Rosalie. No one."

"Not even my dad?"

"Especially not your dad. I don't want my mother knowing, okay?"

"She doesn't know?"

"Can you just shut up long enough for me to look? Maybe you should have stayed in the car."

"Okay, I'm shutting up."

He shot me a look with daggers in his eyes. I opened my mouth to apologize, then quickly closed it. I was already on shaky ground with him, I'd better quit while I was ahead.

I had so many questions for him. He was always Shane the hottie, Shane the jock, or Shane the bad boy, and now he was Shane the artist. He was more complicated than I thought.

We didn't speak on the ride back from the store. As soon as we got back home, Shane carried his stuff up to his bedroom. It was days later when I saw him again and everything changed.

~ Seven ~

I had the day off from work and was sitting in the living room reading when he came down the stairs. He was shirtless, so I lifted my book up a little higher and pretended to be reading while I admired his body.

He had a new rose tattoo on his bicep, but that only distracted me a little before my eyes traveled over his chest. My gaze shifted slowly down to his tight abs and followed his happy trail to his low-rise jeans. I didn't need to use my imagination to picture what was in his jeans.

"The view the other day wasn't enough? You know, you're not supposed to look at your brother like that," he said.

Shit!

"I'm...umm...reading," I said. "Besides, you're not my brother."

"Stepbrother, whatever. Same rules apply. Unless you're into that kinky stuff."

He put on a white fitted shirt and rolled up the sleeves as he looked out the window.

"So when does Shane the asshole show up again?" I asked.

"Shane the asshole is always here, never forget that." He shoved his hands into his pockets and tilted his head as he looked at my book. "What crap are you reading?"

"It's none of your business." I slipped the book under a throw pillow.

"That's one of those burning loins books, isn't it? I saw the man titty on the cover. My grandmother used to read those with Fabio dressed as a pirate or whatever." With a few quick steps, he crossed the room and swiped my book out from under the pillow.

"It's not one of those books. It's just romance. Now give me back my book!"

He opened the book and started flipping through the pages. Settling on a page, he started to read, then looked at me with a crooked smile.

"My grandmother didn't read anything like this. This is porn," he said with a laugh.

"Give it back. It is not porn."

I got up from the couch and tried to grab the book out of his hands but he lifted it higher.

"It *is* porn. It has cock in it and right here she's talking about her wet pussy. Do you use this to get off? Does it make your pussy wet?"

I jumped up and snatched it out of his hands, but he caught me as I tried to get away.

"I was reading that," he said as he reached for the book.

As I tried to pull away, I tripped and fell onto the couch, pulling him along with me. I was on my back and he was on top of me. His warm breath was so close it gave me goose bumps and my nipples hardened. I forgot all about the book until he yanked it out of my hands, then sat on the floor and opened it again.

"Where'd that wet pussy go?" he said as he flipped through the pages again.

It's right here.

I smacked him on the head with the throw pillow and sat up.

"Sounds like you need it more than I do," I said.

Shane put the book down and turned towards me. His intense green eyes locked in with mine.

"How badly do you need it?" he asked as he cocked an eyebrow at me.

He wasn't talking about the book. Even I wasn't stupid enough to think that. Like flipping a switch, my body reacted to his words.

I need it bad. My body throbbed its answer from between my legs.

A car pulled into the driveway and Shane peeked out the window. He held up my book with a crooked smile.

"If you need it, you know where to find me," he said.

With the book in his hands, he went up to his bedroom. I wanted my book back, and I wanted more of whatever just happened. I was about to go after him when my dad entered the house.

"You and Shane will have to fend for yourselves tonight, Rosalie," Dad said. "Joanna has a late meeting and I have to get back to school for parent-teacher conferences." He dug into his wallet, pulled out some cash, and placed it by the phone. "That should be enough for dinner."

"Thanks, Dad. Do you want me to order something for you?"

"No, don't worry about me. Sorry about telling you at the last minute."

Shortly after my dad vanished into his bedroom, I heard the water for the shower start. I went upstairs and was going to get my book back from Shane but saw his bedroom door was closed. Knowing how sensitive I was about my own privacy, I knocked on the door.

After waiting a minute, I gave up. Shane obviously didn't want to be bothered again. I walked back to my room, opened the door, and found Shane sitting on my bed reading. It brought back everything from my stepfather. I wanted him gone.

"What are you doing in here?" I said angrily. "I didn't say you could enter my room. Get out!"

"Get out? Am I not allowed in the princess's room?"

"Just go. Get out! How dare you just come into my room without asking."

"You got a problem with my being in here? Don't tell me you never dreamed about having me in your bedroom." He stood from the bed, the book still in his hand, and glared at me. "I know you want it and it has nothing to do with your fucking porn. I've seen how you look at me. I bet you're wet right now thinking about it."

For a moment I was too stunned to do anything, but my anger took over and I went after him.

"Don't talk to me that way," I said.

"What? Did I get your panties in a bunch? Or does it bother you that even now despite how angry you are at me, your nipples are saluting me?"

I folded my arms over my chest. Stupid body. I couldn't help how my body reacted towards him. It betrayed me every time he was near.

"Get out now! And leave my book," I said.

"I don't want your ridiculous book."

He threw the book onto the bed and stormed past me into the hall. I slammed the door shut as he left, thankful that my tears didn't start until after he was gone.

I didn't know how much time had passed, but the sun had started to set when I heard the doorbell ring. I peeked out my bedroom window and saw the Palermo's delivery van parked in front of the house. Just seeing the car made me realize how hungry I was. Palermo's was my favorite restaurant, and I wondered if Shane knew and was enough of an asshole to not order anything for me.

I left my bedroom, closing the door behind me like I always did. Shane was seated at the dining room table eating pizza.

"Can I have some of your pizza?" I asked.

"No, get your own food."

"You could've told me you were ordering dinner."

He didn't answer. He kept his eyes on me, that same look from school where I felt like he was seeing me naked as he shoved a slice into his mouth and took a big bite.

I folded my arms over my breasts, trying to hide myself from his x-ray vision, and entered the kitchen. On the counter was a white bag with Palermo's written across it. A receipt was stapled to the bag, and 'Rosalie' was written on it.

As I opened the bag, the smell of garlic knots rose up and my mouth watered. Also in the bag was Fettuccine Alfredo with ground sausage, my favorite dish. I grabbed two plates and brought the bag to the dining room.

"Thank you for ordering for me," I said. "Do you want some?"

"Nah, I like their pizza."

We sat in silence while we ate. I caught Shane looking at me every so often, but instead of speaking, he ate more pizza. For once, I didn't want to talk. I didn't want to mess up this moment.

Shane finished his pizza and stared at me. Anytime I looked up, his gaze was still there. He wouldn't stop and I wasn't sure if I wanted him to until I felt myself blushing.

"Do I have Alfredo all over my face?" I asked.

I reached for a napkin and his hand closed over mine.

"I'm sorry about before," he said, his voice husky.

"Just forget about it."

"No, I should know better. When I was in jail, if someone entered my space I would've kicked their ass."

"I overreacted. I'm sensitive about my room, my space. I can't help it."

"Is that why you're here?" he asked.

I nodded.

"You don't have to say anything else. I understand."

He squeezed my hand and somehow I knew he really did understand.

"About what you said in my room..."

"Again, I'm sorry," he said. "I thought maybe something was going on between us and I stupidly thought we could continue it."

"I'd be lying if I said I wasn't thinking the same thing."

"Well, we can't. Not here, not in this house. Not where I'm your stepbrother."

"Then let's go somewhere else."

We decided to head into New Brunswick where there were several large hotels and enough people that no one would notice us. On the ride there, Shane pointed to a 7-Eleven convenience store and asked me to pull in. He came back out after a few minutes with a grocery bag full of stuff.

"What did you get?" I asked, trying to peek into the bag.

"Essentials." He swatted my hand away. "Now keep driving."

The hotel was one of the tallest buildings in the city and overlooked the river. We had no problem getting a room and rode up the glass elevator in silence. My heart was pounding in my chest. I had never done anything like this before, but the thought of being alone in a room with Shane and nothing else but a bed was too good to pass up.

As the elevator doors opened, Shane took my hand and we followed the numbers to our room. He flicked on the lights and set the grocery bag down on the desk next to the television.

In the center of the room was a king-sized bed with brown and cream colored sheets. It faced a wall of windows that were covered with long drapes.

I was beginning to feel awkward, like some kind of slut. I sat on the edge of the bed and wrung my hands together. Shane sat beside me, pushed my hair over my shoulder, and whispered huskily in my ear.

"I know what you want."

His voice gave me chills and my nerves slipped away. I turned to him, hoping he would kiss me again, but instead he stood up and started emptying the bag from the convenience store. I was beyond confused.

"What are you doing?" I asked.

"I know what you want," he said, his voice different from just a minute ago. "Ice cream."

He held up several pints of Ben and Jerry's ice cream and a box of plastic spoons, balanced them in his arms, grabbed the television remote, and set them down on one of the nightstands next to the bed.

"Let's go," he said as he patted the head of the bed. "Get your ass up here."

He propped up some pillows and took off his boots before leaning back against the headboard. I kicked off my sneakers and sat cross-legged beside him.

"Do you have cookie dough?"

"Of course. It's your favorite," he said as he handed me a pint.

"How do you know that? And my favorite from Palermo's too. How did you guess that?"

"I didn't guess, I know," he said. "Your father talks about you a lot and I have to say I enjoy listening. When I was in jail, I didn't have much else to do besides listen."

"I didn't think this was what you were getting when you went to the 7-Eleven."

"What did you think I was getting? Condoms?"

"Actually, yes," I said, laughing.

"I got those too." His face got serious and he leaned in closer to me. "I'd be lying if I said I didn't want to do you right now. But this isn't how I imagined it."

I was stunned. The guy I had been crazy about had imagined having sex with me?

"You imagine it with everyone, don't you?"

"No," he scoffed. "I know what my rep at school was and there was a reason for that. I've had my fair share of pussy, but it all stopped when I saw you."

"You are so full of it."

"Here's the thing, Rosalie. You are too good for me. My life is so fucked up and you've got a future ahead of you."

"What are you talking about?"

"I'm talking about us. We can't happen. I'm a fucking black cat. I'm nothing but bad luck. Everything I do gets fucked sideways. Remember that day when our parents announced they were married? I had seen you before then, before I even said anything to you. It's my fucking bad luck that you became my stepsister. And what happened with Seth was more of my bad luck, too."

"Well, I sometimes think I'm pretty lucky, so maybe we'll cancel each other out," I said.

"You can't be that lucky or you wouldn't have left your mom."

"Why did you leave your mom?"

He lowered his head and shoved a spoonful of ice cream into his mouth.

"You want the CliffsNotes version?" he asked.

"No, I want to know everything."

A pained expression passed over his face. He let out a long sigh, then shook his head.

"I can't tell you everything," he said. "Don't ask why, I just can't right now."

His eyes pleaded with me to understand and I nodded, afraid of saying anything that would silence him.

"I'm sure your dad told you about my pop. We were really close and what's funny is you and I even met when we were kids, when my parents were still together, but I know you don't remember that. You had a doll with you and you both had on matching tiaras."

I laughed. "I remember that doll. I used to take her everywhere."

"I was a stupid kid, it's no wonder you don't remember me. I thought you were a princess, like a real princess. You were so pretty and you had that tiara. We were probably around six and I was too afraid to talk to you then."

"Hmm, six. That explains a lot."

"What do you mean?"

"I don't remember much from when I was six. Well, I remember one thing, in a parking lot, and I don't know if it's real or not. Anyway, forget about it. We're not talking about me."

"We are, why do you think I call you princess?" he said with a crooked smile.

"You usually call me that when you're pissed off."

"I call you that when I'm pissed you're my sister."

It was my turn to look away. I had never blushed so much in my life, but it seemed Shane had that effect on me. It was a little embarrassing.

"So like I said, my pop and I were close. He used to take me everywhere. I don't think my mother ever knew what to do with a boy so she didn't care. My dad had a problem though. He was an addict."

"Is that how you got involved with drugs?"

"Kinda. I was never an addict like my pop. I never used other than smoking some pot once in a blue moon. I saw what it did to people and I didn't want anything to do with it. But sometimes you just don't have a choice."

Ten Years Ago

"Get out!" Joanna screamed. "You lost your job, you spent all of our savings, and now I find out you're dealing? What about Shane? Did you get him involved too? No, don't answer that. I don't want to know. Just get out, Ryan. I'm done. I've had it."

My mother stormed out of the room, leaving my father crying with his face in his hands. I was only eight, but I knew a lot more about adult things than my peers. Cautiously, I put my hand on my father's shoulder.

"Is there anything I can do, Pop?" I asked.

He shook his head. "I don't know, Shane. I don't know. I messed up bad, but there's nothing I can do about it now. Your mother wants me gone. You have to make a choice, are you coming with me or staying here?"

I didn't see it as a choice; my father needed me, my mother didn't. I saw how things were when I was around, I was nothing but a thorn in her side.

"Where will we go?" I asked.

"To your grandmother's in Philly. She'll take us in. Don't tell your mother though."

"Why not?"

"Because your mother and grandmother don't get along."

I had only seen my grandmother a handful of times, and most of them were when we picked her up at the train station during a visit. We never went to visit her in Philly and that day I found out why.

Grandma Ventana, or Abuela as she wanted me to call her, lived in the ghetto. The buildings around her were in disrepair. Some of them looked condemned with boarded-up windows, but people still lived in them.

Abuela's home was off an unmaintained street in a forgotten part of the city. The brick tenements were so close to each other that some leaned against the others. The air had a bad combination of filth and decay.

The wide sidewalk in front of her house was busy. Hanging between the buildings over the street were electrical wires and clotheslines with shoes dangling by their laces. I soon learned the hanging shoes was a sign that drugs were sold in that area.

Abuela sat in a rickety lawn chair in front of her building. She stood as we walked up the street from the train station, her head shaking with disappointment.

"*Sinvergüenza*," she said, looking at my father. "It's the drugs, isn't it? Get inside and I'll make you something to eat."

As Abuela fried drumsticks, my dad and I sat at the large dining room table. The room was painted a bright orange and a large crucifix hung on one of the walls.

When they were done, she placed the chicken on the table with a pile of paper plates, then sat down. My father started eating like he had never seen food before in his life. Abuela clucked her tongue as she shook her head.

"So you're my problem now, huh?" she said.

"I'm sorry, Mami, but I had nowhere else to go," Pop said.

"This is my fault. I didn't watch you enough when you were younger. I thought I could trust you with the product, instead you started using." She clucked her tongue before running it over her teeth.

"You'll have to work for me again, but this time if anything's missing, you're paying double for it."

"Yes, Mami, whatever you want."

Her eyes turned towards me and she squinted through her glasses.

"How old are you now?" she asked.

"I'm eight."

"You look like a bright boy, how'd you like to make some money and help your father out?"

Present Day

"I delivered drugs to Abuela's dealers. Her thinking was that I was a child, a juvenile, so they would be more lenient on me than an adult."

"That's terrible," I said.

"It wasn't as bad as you think. My grandmother and I grew close and I understood why she did what she did. I'd do anything for her, and I proved that by never giving the cops her name."

"So when you had Seth's eyeglass case in school..."

"The cops ran my name and all my priors came up. They had no choice but to take me in and since I wouldn't play ball with them, they locked me up."

"I'm so sorry," I said. "All this time I was worried it was my fault, and it really is."

"Nah, it's just my shit life. I can't get away from it. Abuela passed away a couple of years ago. That's when Pop and I moved and I started going to your school. I could have told the cops what they wanted to know, but I didn't want to disrespect her memory."

He was quiet and he gave me that look again where I thought he could see through my clothes. Only this time it didn't bother me. This time I knew he was seeing something more.

"Right now," he said. "Right here, tonight, this has been the best day of my fucked-up life. Being in bed with you like this has made all of that shit okay because I know it was bringing me to you."

I was lost in his words. I knew he was being sincere, but part of me couldn't believe it. Why was the guy I stalked in the halls not that long ago saying all these amazing things to me? It was unreal. I couldn't handle how serious he was.

"Is this how you got into all those girls' pants?" I asked with a grin.

"That depends. Is it working?" He tilted his head to the side as he pushed my hair off my shoulder. "You don't like being serious, do you? It makes you uncomfortable."

"Maybe. Or maybe I'm just nervous because I think I know what's about to happen."

"Do you?"

His hand cupped my face and pulled me closer. His kiss was gentle at first, then more demanding. As his tongue slid near my tongue, I moaned softly.

"I like that," he said. "Do it again."

"I can't. It just happened."

"Then I'm going to make it happen again."

"I don't think you can."

"I love a challenge," he said.

He moved further down on the bed so we were lying next to each other. His lips kissed my neck before he pressed them against mine. He sucked on my bottom lip and bit it. I forced myself to not make a sound.

"Nothing? We'll see about that," he said with a crooked smile.

"What are you going to do?"

"I'm going to make you moan so loud the people in the next room will complain."

I laughed as he pulled me against him until I felt his hard cock pressed against my thigh. The memory of him naked drifted through my mind. I pressed myself against him more, then slid my hand over him.

"You make me so fucking hard. Do you have any idea how hard it is to think with you in the next room? To hear the shower turn on and to imagine you naked?"

"I want to see you again," I said, lifting his shirt.

He pulled his shirt off quickly then unbuttoned his jeans and kicked them off. Lying naked beside me, he pulled my face to his again, his tongue hungrily exploring my mouth.

His hands moved roughly over my shirt, squeezing my breasts before reaching for my pants. I felt him hesitate a moment before he pulled them down past my hips. I pushed them off then moved my bare leg against his.

Shane reached for my hips and pushed his cock between my legs, against my panties.

"You're so wet I can feel it through your panties," he said.

He groaned as he rubbed his cock against the thin material. His hands grabbed my ass, pressing me tightly against him.

"I can't take it anymore. Please just fuck me already," I said. I started to pull my panties down, but he stopped me.

"No, we can't. I want you so fucking bad, but we can't."

"It's because I'm your stepsister, isn't it?"

"That's only part of it," he said. "I wasn't joking when I said today has been the best day of my life. And if we did this right now, I could die a happy man. But I can't do it. I keep waiting for something bad to happen. Nothing this good ever happens to me. You're too good for me. I know something will fuck this up just like everything else in my life."

I wanted to argue with him and tell him nothing would happen, but I couldn't. I didn't have the words to make him feel better. And I didn't want to say something to ruin what wasn't just the best day of his life, but mine too.

We spent hours lying in bed together, Shane naked and me still in my shirt and panties. The time flew by as we kissed and touched each other, but we never let it go too far.

~ Eight ~

The next few days were a blur. Shane didn't come out of his room much, and when he did, he kept to himself. He hardly looked at me and I knew he was avoiding me.

I found myself falling on my old high school habits. I looked for little clues and signs of what he was doing or where he had been. He went out several times, but I didn't know who he was with. *Was he dating?* Just the thought of it made my chest ache.

Shane would come out of his room late, after everyone had fallen asleep, but whenever I tried to talk to him, he disappeared back into his room without a word. Part of me was glad he wasn't yelling at me, but another part wished he was. I needed something from him, even if it was him being mean. The silence was worse than almost anything he could possibly say.

The rest of the house was asleep and I knew Shane would be up soon to eat or whatever it was he did in the middle of the night. I had to stop listening for him and thinking about him. I had to stop obsessing about him. Needing something to get my mind off him, I looked at my cell phone and decided to see what Noelle had been up to.

"Hey stranger," she said as she answered.

"Thanks, that makes me feel even better."

"Nah, you know I'm just busting your chops. I haven't been around much lately either with getting ready to go away and trying to spend as much time with Craig as possible."

"How are things with him?"

"Things are...well, they could be better. You know when we started dating the whole plan was we were just hanging out for the summer. No strings, no ties since we were both going away. But now it's different and that's making it harder. He's even talking about transferring to my school, but I told him that's just insane. What's going on with you? How's Shane, your way-hot stepbrother? Have you accidentally walked in on him in the shower yet?"

I laughed. "No, but now you're giving me more ideas. I guess he's alright. I don't think he's talking to me right now, which is a bummer. I'm trying to not think about it though."

"Okay, then I'll change the subject. Have you heard from your mom?"

"No. I called her a week or so ago, but she never called me back. She's pissed at me. She hasn't spoken to me since the day I left and that day she said something about my betraying her."

"Sorry, I'm sure that's got to be hard."

"Yeah, but you know what? I feel so much more at ease not being there. I think I'm okay with it. She's just going to be how she is. I can't let it affect me. Now if only the nightmares would stop."

"The parking lot nightmares?"

"Yup, those. They go away for a while and then come back."

"It's better that you're not there and you know that. Jim was such a creep, and I hated visiting you. And now that Shane lives there, I really should be coming over more often."

"Shut up," I said, laughing. "See, I missed this. I missed talking to you."

"I missed it too. And I'm going to miss you once I leave, but now that you're out of that house you could visit on break and maybe we can do something on spring break. It'll be nice to have a best friend I can actually do things with."

"Thanks, rub it in."

"Aww, you know it's just because I love you."

"Love you too, Noelle."

"It's late, I'm gonna crash. Call me tomorrow."

As I got off the phone, I decided to give in to sleep. I turned on my favorite playlist and as the music played, I closed my eyes.

***

"Rosalie," Shane hissed. "Wake up."

I gasped for air as my eyes flew open. Shane was wearing nothing but black boxer briefs.

"What the fuck?" I said as I pulled my blanket up. "Get the fuck out of my room!"

"Calm down," he said, holding his hands out. "I heard you crying. You sounded really upset and when you didn't answer, I came in. Are you alright?"

I nodded, then burst into tears and shook my head. Sitting up, I pulled my legs up to me and then grabbed my pillow. Shane sat beside me and wrapped his arms around me.

"Nightmare?" he asked.

I nodded, unable to speak. He didn't ask anything else, but I couldn't shake the visions from my mind. I never told anyone how the nightmare related to my oldest memory. I couldn't say the words, and it wouldn't matter because none of it made any sense. But for whatever reason, I wanted to tell Shane.

As I looked up at him, he met my gaze and pushed my hair back from my face.

"Can I tell you about it?" I asked. "I don't know if it'll make any sense, but I think I need to talk about it."

"You can tell me anything."

I took a deep breath and closed my eyes for a moment, feeling safe in his arms.

"I've been having these nightmares since I was little. In the dreams I'm around five or six. I'm scared and hiding behind cars in a parking lot in the apartment complex we used to live in when I was little. The dream always ends with me being grabbed from behind and my screaming."

"Did it really happen? Because I have nightmares of things that happened to me."

"I don't know. I wish I knew. I asked my mother about it once. I told her about the dream and she told me that Jim once found me wandering in the parking lot behind his apartment. This was before they started dating and he was her boss. He told her I was cutting school, but I always remember loving school."

"Do you remember him finding you?"

"No, I don't. My memory of that morning is fragmented. I remember him on the phone, I was standing with my book bag near the front door, and I remember the rocking chair next to me was rocking."

"That's it?"

"That's it. When I asked my mom if she remembered anything from that day, all she said was that I changed after that and I wasn't the happy kid I used to be."

"What do you think happened?"

"I don't know," I said. "I don't think I want to know. I just wish the nightmares would stop."

He held me tightly as I clung to him. I didn't know how much time had passed, but he slowly let me go and wiped a stray tear from my cheek.

"I'd better get back to bed," he said.

"Please don't. I'm afraid to fall asleep. Can you stay here with me?"

Shane's eyes told me how much he was wrestling with what I said. I knew how he felt about being my stepbrother when we were living together like this, but I didn't feel that way. It was just another term for him no different than my dad calling him a bad boy. Shane was my stepbrother bad boy, but they were just words to me.

"I don't know," he said softly. "It's hard enough to be near you like this. And you're so vulnerable and sad right now, I'm afraid of doing something and taking advantage of you. That's the last thing I want to do."

"You could never take advantage of me. If anything happens between us, it's because I want it to."

He held my hand and traced the lines of my palm with his finger. His fingertips were covered with dried paint in different colors.

"Were you painting?" I asked.

"Yes. I've never shown anyone before, but do you want to see what I've been working on?"

"I'd love that."

Shane went through our shared bathroom to his room and came back with a painting on a square canvas he bought the week before. It wasn't done, but it already had such rich colors and bold lines to it, I thought it was beautiful.

"I still have a lot of work to do on it, but it's for you. I know your birthday is coming up and despite what a douche I've been at times, you never gave up on me."

"Really? You're making this for me?"

He nodded. "It's a rose, like your name. You're the reason I got this rose on my bicep. It reminds me to stay strong. I've had a lot of thorns in my life, but the thing that has kept me going was knowing one day I'd reach the rose and it would all be worth it. So I kept climbing over the thorns and eventually it brought me here, to you. And now I'm here helping you with this thorn, your nightmare."

I didn't know what to say. I was grateful to have him there with me at that moment, but anything I said would have paled in comparison.

"What about you?" he asked. "I told you I paint to relax, do you have anything like that?"

"I write. I like writing poetry, sometimes short stories."

"I'd love to read your stuff."

"No, you wouldn't like it. It's just...they're stupid stories."

"Don't ever say that. If they mean something to you then they can never be stupid."

I kept waiting for him to make a joke out of it, but he didn't. He was serious. And I knew I was in trouble. I was falling for him.

"How did you learn how to paint?" I asked.

"I'm sure you can guess I had a lot of spare time in jail. There's not much to do besides lifting weights or reading. One day when I was in the library, I picked up a book on modern art and fell in love with Cubism. I started sketching and after I got out, I bought some supplies and experimented."

"That's amazing."

"My grandmother helped. She bought me art magazines and paid for some classes when we were living with her. Then one day I discovered this artist named Dmitri Nikita. His work is incredible and it really inspired me. I'd love to go to his studio in California and meet him one day. Maybe take a class from him."

"I always dreamed about going to California."

"We should go, just you and me. We could get away from the bad weather and the nightmares. Just leave all this crap behind."

I searched his face looking for some joke I didn't get, but there wasn't one there. I leaned against Shane, grateful to have him there to keep my thorns away. The more time we spent together, the more I felt myself falling for him, my stepbrother. Was it wrong? He was everything I wanted, but the one I couldn't have. *Or could I?*

~ Nine ~

Even though I had started college, it didn't feel any different or special like I had hoped it would. I knew the problem was that I was a commuter. Everyone in my classes seemed to live in the dorm and had made tons of friends, but I didn't meet anyone. In a lot of ways, college was no different than high school since no one knew I was alive.

The big difference though was that I didn't care. I wanted to go away to college to get out of my house with my mother and stepfather. I did that by moving in with my dad. And with Shane living there, I didn't want to date or meet anyone else.

I was finishing up a paper for an assignment when my phone started ringing. Shane's name floated across the screen.

"Why are you calling me if you're in the next room?" I said.

"Hi, is Rosalie there?" he said.

"Huh? What are you doing? You know it's me."

"How you doin'? Are you busy tonight?"

"I thought we were going to rent a movie," I said.

"Fuck, Rosalie, can't you take a hint? I'm trying to ask you out."

Holy shit!

"So, are you busy tonight?" he asked.

"I was going to rent a movie tonight with my stepbrother."

"Ditch the loser and come out with me."

"What did you have in mind?"

"Just the usual wine 'em, dine 'em, sixty-nine 'em."

"You're an asshole, you know that?"

"Yeah, but you love me anyway."

I do.

"So what do you say?"

"Yes, I'll go out with you tonight."

"I'll pick you up at seven."

"Do you know where I live?" I held back a giggle.

"Of course I do. Your stepbrother told me."

***

The doorbell rang at exactly seven o'clock. My dad and Joanna had left earlier for a dinner party with some friends, so I was alone in the house except for Shane. It felt silly, but I wore my favorite dress. Shane called it a date and I was going to make sure I looked my best.

"Shane! Can you get that?" I yelled.

Shane didn't respond. Instead, the doorbell rang again. *Who the hell is ringing the doorbell?* I ran down the stairs with my shoes in my hand and yanked the door open. Shane was standing on the other side of the door with a wide grin.

"Hey gorgeous," he said.

"What are you doing?"

"I told you I would pick you up at seven. Don't tell me you're not ready yet."

"Shut up and get back in here. Where are we going?"

"I'm going to give you two choices. We can go out and do the dinner and a movie thing, or we can stay here."

"That's it? I'm disappointed. I expected you to say something crude."

"Well, if you're interested, my fucking your brains out could be option number three."

"There it is," I said, laughing. "Actually I was looking forward to staying home and renting a movie."

"Score! I have a cheap date!" He laughed. "How about ordering from Palermo's?"

"That would be perfect."

I changed into a pair of jeans and a t-shirt and after eating dinner, we went to the living room, sat on the couch, and watched a couple of movies. I didn't feel like we were on a date, it felt normal and natural even though we rarely spent time in the house together.

"So, I'm a little confused," I said.

"What about? Zoolander is a male model," he said slowly, enunciating each word.

"Not that, you jerk. I thought you didn't want anything to happen between us."

"Right, I *do* lie naked with all of my sisters." Shane pulled my feet up, put them on his lap, and stroked my leg.

"It's a good thing you're an only child then."

"Seriously though, I've been doing a lot of thinking about us. I hear in certain places it's perfectly normal to screw around with your sister, so maybe we should give it a try."

"I can't believe I agreed to go on a date with you." I shook my head. "You're a child."

He turned off the television and turned to face me, his eyes looking into me like only he could. I thought about our night at the hotel and turned away from his stare in case he could read my mind.

"I know what you're thinking about. I haven't forgotten about that night either," he said, his voice husky. "Or any night I've slept in the room next to yours. You're all I think about, Rosalie, whether you're my stepsister or not." He stood and opened the front door. "I don't know what's right anymore. But please do me a favor and go to your room and lock your door. Your skin is so damn soft, just touching your leg gave me a hard on. I don't want to do anything I might regret."

He stepped outside and I stood to follow him, then stopped myself. I didn't want to be a regret of his.

I went to my bedroom and, like he asked, I locked my door. After getting ready for bed, I lay in the dark and stared up at the ceiling as I listened to the house.

The shutter outside my window creaked as the wind blew. A car drove past. Shane's footsteps echoed in the hall as he went to his room. I lost track of time, but none of it mattered because all I could think about was his naked body lying against me. I covered my face with a pillow as I tried to suffocate myself to sleep.

Tap tap tap.

What was that? I pushed the pillow aside and waited, but didn't hear anything. Probably a squirrel in the attic.

Tap tap tap.

I knew what the sound was that time. I got up and stood in front of the closed bathroom door.

"Shane?" I whispered.

Tap tap tap.

I opened the door. Shane was shirtless but still in his jeans. He grabbed my face with his hands and pressed his lips against mine. I threw my arms around his neck and as he picked me up, I wrapped my legs around his waist.

As he lay me on the bed, he pushed his jeans off and they dropped to the floor. His body looked even more cut in the moonlight. Pulling the blanket back, I slid over and he got into bed with me.

"You changed your mind?" I asked.

"Shh. You talk too much." He smiled then kissed me again. "I don't care whose house this is, I don't care if you're my stepsister, I just want to be with you."

He pulled my nightshirt up and threw it aside as he kissed my shoulder and pressed me against his rock-hard body as we lay on our sides. My hands wandered over him, feeling the strong muscles of his back, down to his firm butt.

As I leaned back onto the bed, his lips found mine and he kissed me deeply. His hand moved over my breast and I arched my body, pressing myself further into his palm, wanting more. All my inhibitions drifted away as his fingers moved over the curve of my body to my hip, where his fingers ran across the edge of my panties.

"Are you okay with this?" he asked.

"Yes," I said, panting, wondering if he stopped to torture me.

His fingers curled around the edge of my bikini. I gazed back into his intense eyes as I slid my hand down to his hard cock. I moved my hand slowly up and down his shaft as he slowly pulled my panties down. He was definitely some kind of sadist.

My body trembled as his lips brushed over my breasts before taking a nipple into his mouth. He sucked on it slowly, then rougher, brushing his teeth against the hard nubbin before treating the other one the same way. I moaned as my body pulsed with desire.

"I don't know, I'm not getting the sense you really want it."

I slid my hand a little faster on his cock, but he stopped me and shook his head, scolding me. My panties moved down further and I lifted my legs out of them. I was ready to jump him. He moved his hand over my mound.

"How badly do you need it?" he asked with a sly grin.

"Are you really going to make me beg?"

"Maybe I want to hear how badly you want me inside your wet pussy."

He slid a finger into my wetness and I was quickly close to the edge. All the dirty talk and time spent with him over the past few weeks had been like foreplay for me.

"Please," I breathed.

He reached down to his jeans and pulled out a condom. Ripping the package open with his teeth, he pulled it out and swiftly rolled it over his thick rod.

His lips closed over mine as his cock rubbed over my wetness. I felt the pressure of his tip against my entrance as he continued to kiss me. His cock thrust inside my pussy and I moaned.

"You're so fucking tight," he groaned before moving his hips faster.

Each movement pushed me closer towards the edge. There was nothing sweet about what we were doing at that moment, it was pure lust and desire. A moan escaped my lips.

"I love making you moan," he said.

He pulled my thigh up, entering me deeper. The sweat of our bodies made us slicker. I was ready to cry out his name when I heard the door open downstairs.

"Shit, they're home," I said. "We're going to get caught."

"Not if we're quiet."

He slowed his pumping as our parents entered the house. While the thought of getting caught worried me at first, Shane continued his long thrusts into me and got me more excited.

"I'm close," I whispered.

As his cock thrust into me faster, I heard our parents as they walked down the hall past my door. My pussy tightened around Shane and his mouth closed over mine as the wave of release hit me.

I moaned, but his kiss silenced me. As my body quivered underneath him, he gasped into the pillow behind me, thrusting as he came.

We lay panting in each other's arms, the moonlight glistening against our bodies. Hearing our parents' bedroom door finally close, we both let out a sigh and laughed.

He kissed me tenderly as he stroked my arm. As I looked into his eyes, I wondered if he felt the same way I did. I wasn't falling for Shane anymore, I had already fallen hard.

~ Ten ~

For months, our Saturday night routine was bringing dinner to the hotel and staying there until we thought we should head home. We didn't always have sex, the hotel wasn't really for that. We went to the hotel so we could be together without having to worry what anyone else would think.

Neither of us knew what our parents would say about our being together. Joanna didn't seem to notice anything, but I had a feeling my dad was suspicious. Having to pretend Shane meant nothing to me while all I could think about was lying in his arms got harder as the months went by.

The hotel room was dark except for the glow from the television. Shane held me as we watched an old movie. Our legs were tangled together under the sheets and my head lay on his bare chest. I loved being naked with Shane, it felt so natural. I didn't feel self-conscious or uncomfortable about my body. If anything, I felt beautiful.

I let out a long sigh as the movie ended. It was after midnight and we would have to go back home and back to pretending.

"What was that for?" Shane asked.

"What?"

"That sigh. Is something wrong?"

"No, everything's great. I just hate having to leave here."

"I know, I do too. I'd give anything to be your boyfriend seven days a week instead of just one night."

I looked up at him and he leaned towards me, pushing me onto the pillow. His mouth closed over mine and I pressed my body closer to his. As our tongues met, I was reminded of the time and what the next day was. I pulled away and smiled softly at him.

"What's wrong? There's something else, isn't there?"

"I have to go to my mother's tomorrow. She called me the other day and said she was cleaning out the house and that if I didn't get my stuff, she was tossing it. Most of the things she has are from when I was little and I don't care about them. But she has my princess doll. I don't want to go there, but I have to get that doll."

"I can go with you," he said.

"Really? You would?"

"Of course. You know I'd do anything for you."

***

The next morning, I pulled my car up to the curb in front of my mother's house. It had been over six months since I had last been there, but all the dread came back as if it was yesterday. Shane must have seen my hesitation because he put his hand over mine on the steering wheel and gently squeezed.

"I'm here," he said. "Nothing bad will happen."

We got out of the car and walked up the driveway to the house. It was quiet and there weren't any cars in the driveway.

"I don't think anyone's home," I said.

I rang the doorbell and when no one answered, I put my key in the lock and opened the door. Several boxes with my name on them were stacked near the entrance.

"Let's just take them all," I said. "I can go through them at home. I'll leave my mom a note to let her know I was here."

As Shane carried the boxes out to the car, my mother pulled into the driveway. I was still in the house writing a note when she came inside.

"Good, you found your things," she said coldly. "I think that's everything. I accidentally threw out some of your boxes, so this is all that's left."

"Thanks, Mom."

I didn't know how to act with her. She was always hot and cold with me, and I didn't want to say something wrong and have to deal with her anger.

There was one box left. I wondered what happened to Shane and then I realized my mother wasn't alone. Ice ran through my veins as I looked outside and saw Jim talking to Shane. Even from inside the house, I could tell Jim was trying to intimidate Shane.

He kept stepping closer to him, closing the distance between them as he spoke. Jim's hand was up and he poked Shane in the shoulder, then pointed back at the house. Shane's eyes were narrowing and his fists clenched at his sides.

I grabbed the last box and bumped the door open with my hip. As I stepped outside, I could hear Jim's voice, but I couldn't make out the words except for the last one.

"...cunt," Jim said.

Shane's fist connected with Jim's face. Jim fell to the ground, his hands over his nose. Blood began to seep down his face as he glared at Shane.

Shane's eyes were wild like an animal ready to attack. I shoved the last box into Shane's hands as he stood over Jim, but it wasn't enough. His eyes were glued on Jim. I knew he was waiting for him to make another move.

"Let's go," I said.

I grabbed Shane's arm and pulled. His eyes shifted to me briefly, then back at Jim. He stepped back, put the box inside the trunk, and then got into the car. I drove away as quickly as I could.

My body began to shake and I couldn't focus on the road. My dad only lived a block away, but I was too confused to get there. I stopped the car in front of the neighborhood park.

"Are you okay?" Shane asked.

"I'll be fine. I'm just shaken up."

Shane's hands cupped my face as he looked into my eyes.

"I'm sorry I lost it back there," he said. "That guy is a fucking asshole. He's lucky all I did was punch him."

"What happened? I was leaving a note for my mom when she came into the house."

"Your stepfather got out of the car and asked if I was your new boyfriend. I told him I was your stepbrother and he said it didn't matter who I was. That he was going to warn me about you."

"Warn you?"

"Yeah, warn me about how irresponsible and lazy you are and all sorts of other things. He was just talking smack. I know you were supporting them, he probably thought I didn't know anything."

"He said more than that, didn't he?"

"I don't want to tell you."

"Tell me. I need to know."

"He was talking about how pretty you were. Then he said..."

"Tell me. I think I know what he said. I heard the last word."

"He misses the smell of your..."

"Cunt," I said. "It was something my mother used to say to me. Well, kind of. She used to say that she hated me and that I was a slut and that men could smell me like a dog in heat."

"She's a fucking bitch."

"Sorry you had to hear all of that. At least it got us out of there quick." I smiled.

"You're taking it well."

"I'm used to it, unfortunately. But it's one of the reasons why I left. I couldn't take it there anymore and I think after this I'm going to promise myself to never see him again." Just the promise alone was enough to put me at ease. "Can you tell me something though? What did it feel like to punch him?"

"After what he was saying about you, he deserved more than just a punch. But it did feel good."

"I bet it did. I've always wanted to punch him, beat him, clobber him with a two-by-four."

"And they call me a bad boy," he said with a laugh. "I think that makes you a bad girl. I'll have to remember that for next Saturday." He cocked his brow at me with a half smile.

"Mmm, I'll make sure to remind you."

***

Later that afternoon, I heard Shane out front talking to a man I didn't recognize. The man was tall with broad shoulders in a brown suit. By his stance and demeanor, he looked like a cop. I stayed inside by the window so I could eavesdrop.

"I'm sorry, Paul, I lost my cool," Shane said. "He was pushing all the buttons. He's lucky I only punched him."

"No, you're lucky you only punched him," Paul said. "I talked him into not pressing charges, but what happens next time?"

"There won't be a next time."

"You need to get away from here. Maybe go somewhere and start fresh."

"I can't," Shane said. "I'm not going anywhere without her."

Paul shook his head. "She'd better be worth it because I don't know if you'll be this lucky next time. You've gotten into trouble twice already because of her."

"This guy deserved it."

"Doesn't matter, he's not the one on parole. Move away, go to college, do something other than stay here. You say the word and I can make arrangements for you somewhere else. You're a good kid, you just need the right chance. Think about it."

Paul got into his car and left. Shane lit a cigarette, the first one I had seen him smoke in a long time, and took a deep drag from it. I wanted to go out and talk to him, but I figured it was better to leave him alone. I had already caused enough trouble for him.

~ Eleven ~

It had been almost a week since I overheard Shane talking to Paul. Every day I wanted to ask him about what he said, but I knew if I waited until Saturday night we'd be able to talk more freely.

We were eating dinner in the hotel room, a pizza we brought with us, when I couldn't take it anymore. I had to tell him what I overheard.

"I heard you talking to that Paul guy last week," I said.

"You did? He's my parole officer. Why didn't you say anything?"

I shrugged. "I don't know. I guess I was waiting to see if you'd say anything."

"How much did you hear?"

"He thinks you should go away."

"Doesn't matter what he thinks. I don't want to."

"Because of me?"

"Listen, I know he's right. I know Jersey is bad news for me. The old Shane would have and did blame you for my bad luck, but it's not your fault."

"Then you should go. Don't stay here just because of me."

My heart ached as I spoke. I didn't want him to leave.

"You are the best reason to do anything," he said. "I'm not going anywhere without you. I even told Warren that."

"Warren? From high school?"

The guy you said I was no one to?

"Yeah, from high school. Ends up he's moving out west. He's going to Arizona and asked if I wanted to go too. He's got a U-Haul for all his shit and a friend who'll let us crash until we find a place."

"Are you thinking about going?"

"No, like I said, I'm not going anywhere without you. You need to finish school, that's important. How else are you going to be a famous writer?"

I can be a writer anywhere, I thought. I didn't say it though because I couldn't help but think I was keeping Shane from having his own life. Paul was right, I had been nothing but trouble for him.

"When is Warren leaving?"

"Probably tomorrow, Monday at the latest. Anyway, it's a non-issue."

Would Shane be better off somewhere else? Was Paul right? Would he have a better life away from me? I wanted to shove my head in the sand and not think about it.

"Let's talk about something else," I said.

"Sure, whatever you want." His hands moved up my body as he kissed my neck. "You feel tense. Let me help you relax."

With his arms around me, he brought me to the bed. He slowly undressed me, kissing each part of me as he revealed it. His lips moved so tenderly, I wondered if he was thinking the same thing I was about his leaving.

His caresses were gentle, less demanding than the other times we had been together. He held me close as he kissed me deeply. I clung to him, wishing he would never let me go.

Silently, he put the condom on and slipped back into my embrace. With his eyes locked on mine, I felt the pressure of his cock against my entrance. His lips claimed mine as he thrust his cock into me. As he slowly pumped his hips, he continued to kiss me, only stopping to gaze into my eyes.

This time was different. While sex had never been as wanton or lustful as our first time together, it was never this deliberate. With each thrust I felt more emotion. Our first time we fucked, other times we had sex, but this time we were making love.

***

Shane's chest rose and fell steadily as he slept. It was still early enough that we didn't need to go, but I couldn't relax enough to sleep. All I could do was think about what Shane said earlier and the advice he got from Paul.

It was too much of a coincidence that Warren was leaving tomorrow, it was like fate was saying it was time for him to leave. Arizona wasn't where Shane wanted to go, but it would get him closer to his goal of California.

After such a horrible life with his grandmother and everything that stemmed from that, he needed a new start. And he needed it without me.

As I lay in the dimly lit hotel room, I saw how Shane went from doing anything to please his grandmother to doing anything for me. I was grateful for it, but it didn't feel right. He needed to be on his own and do things for himself.

Paul was right, in one year I managed to get him in jail once and almost back in a second time. Maybe we just weren't meant to be.

Thinking about letting him go made my chest ache. I didn't want to lose him, but maybe it was for the best. If Shane wasn't going to think about himself and what was good for him, then I would. I had to end it with him so he could have the life he deserved.

~ Twelve ~

It was after midnight when Shane woke. As he stretched beside me, I watched his muscles ripple. I put my hand on his abs, over his six-pack, then slid my fingers up onto his chest as he yawned.

This might be the last time I touch you.

"I was thinking about what we were talking about before," he said as he sat up. "This year is almost done for you, maybe you could transfer to a school in California. I can leave with Warren and do some odd jobs and save some money so that everything will be set when you come out."

"Transfer schools? I...I don't know."

It wasn't something I thought of, but it didn't change how I felt. Shane needed to have his own life and to find his own way. He couldn't do that with me around.

"Say you'll come, Rosalie. I don't want to go out there without you. You're the other part of my soul. My entire life has brought me to you. I'm not going without you."

"No, you should do this for yourself. You should go with Warren. Stop thinking about me. You need to be happy."

"You make me happy. I'm nothing without you, why would I leave when you're here?"

"I...can't go. I'm going to finish school here. I can't go with you, Shane."

"What do you mean? What are you saying?"

"I don't know what I'm saying. I just...you should go. Do like Paul said and start a new life, away from me."

"But I love you. All I want to do is be with you," he said.

Those words were something I dreamed about hearing him tell me, something deep down I knew he felt. But I couldn't say the words back to him. If I did, he would never leave. I had to say something so he would go and have the wonderful life he deserved.

"I met someone else," I said.

Even as the words came out of my mouth, I wished I could take them back. He didn't say anything. He stared at me, his eyes piercing through me. I couldn't meet his stare. If I looked at him long enough, he would know I was lying. I turned away from him.

The silence in the room was deafening. Shane got up from the bed and crossed in front of me. His eyes were watery and seeing them felt like a knife slicing through my heart.

He got dressed then tossed my clothes towards me. This was the worst break up I could ever imagine. Not only did I have to ride home in the car with him, but I had to live with him. Or worse, he'd leave hating me.

As he parked the car in front of our house, he looked at me again. His jaw was set and his eyes were still red.

"You cut me to the bone," he said. "I'm leaving tomorrow. I hope that fucking bastard you met knows how special you are."

He slammed the car door shut and went into the house without turning back.

What was I doing? I didn't want him to leave. I wanted to stay with him. But I had to convince myself it was better this way. He was better off without me. I swallowed my tears and stuffed down my emotions.

"I love you too," I whispered.

Shane left in the morning before I woke up. He left a note for his mother letting her know what he was doing and that he'd be in touch. He never said goodbye.

I was broken, wrecked, ruined. His leaving destroyed me, but it was all my doing. Slowly, my heart that always raced whenever Shane was around stopped its frantic rhythm. I drowned myself in my classes and finished college ahead of schedule. I spent years waiting for any sign of Shane, any mention of his name, but there was none.

And then one day, four years later, my father spoke the words that made my heart start pounding again.

"Shane is coming."

PART III

The Heart Never Forgets

~ *Thirteen* ~

Four Years Later

After graduation, I moved to California just like I told Shane I would one day. Not a day went by where I didn't think about him. Despite not seeing him in years, I still remembered the time we spent together like it was yesterday.

My father and Joanna divorced shortly after I finished college, but remained friends. Even when they were together, I never felt comfortable enough to ask her about Shane and she never mentioned him. I dated several guys through college, but none of them could compare to his memory.

I had fallen into the habit of Googling Shane regularly over the years but never found any trace of him. Other than my memories, Shane didn't exist. Despite not finding him even on social media, I still kept hoping I'd get a glimpse of him again and see how he was doing. Did I make the right decision by letting him go?

I knew I needed to get over him, but it was tough. I'd regularly kick myself for having feelings for him still and then one night, while I was out with some friends, I met David. David was nothing like Shane. He was tall and lanky with perfect dark hair that never moved out of place. He was very serious and rarely joked around. He was the complete opposite of my ideal guy, but for some reason, I kept dating him.

David was at my apartment watching a DVD when my phone rang. I reached for the remote to turn the volume down when he swiped it out of my hand.

I looked at the caller ID and was surprised to see my mother's phone number. We hadn't spoken in years despite my calls to her. My old feelings of dread crept back as the phone rang again.

"You going to get that or not?" David said.

"Hello?" I said, answering the phone.

"Rosalie? It's your mother."

"Umm hi, Mom."

I didn't know what to say. Why was she suddenly calling me? I couldn't help but think she wanted something.

"Jim is dying," she said. "He was diagnosed with lung cancer a couple of years ago and it's traveled to his brain. The doctors said he has at most a month to live."

"I'm sorry. Are you okay?"

"I'm fine. He's tough to deal with, very angry, but I've been traveling to keep myself away."

"You've been traveling? Who's taking care of him?"

David glared at me, so I got up from the couch and went into the kitchen.

"He's a grown man, he can take care of himself," she said. "I just got back from a resort in Scottsdale. I can see why you wanted to head west, it's beautiful there."

"You went by yourself?"

"Yes, but I met a friend there."

"Oh? Gladys?"

"No, a new friend, Johnny. We met on Facebook."

"You mean a boyfriend? But what about Jim?"

"I already told you, he's dying. Johnny's really nice, has a big house, and tells me how beautiful I am."

"Umm okay, that's nice, Mom."

Good to see nothing has changed, Mom.

"Anyway, Jim asked me to call you. He wants you to visit here in Florida before he dies. He said he needs to talk to you."

He needs to talk to me? No way. No fucking way.

"No, Mom. I can't. I'm sorry, but I can't do that."

"You've always been an ungrateful person."

"Ungrateful? Did he do something for me to be grateful for? You know how he made me feel. You know the things he did and you never once tried to stop it."

"He was my husband. You always stand by your man."

"Is that what you're doing now with Johnny?"

"That's different. Jim can't perform his husbandly duties anymore."

"I can't believe you, Mom. I really can't believe you."

"So are you coming or not? You can stay here in the guest room."

I shook as I listened to her voice. I never spoke back to her. I was always afraid of the consequences. But hearing her after all these years and realizing that nothing changed set me off.

"Aren't you listening to me? For years I felt like you hated me. I felt like I didn't matter, that all you cared about was pleasing Jim and you didn't care what you sacrificed as long as he was happy. How could you treat your daughter like that? You're my mom, you were supposed to protect me."

I blinked back the few tears that stung my eyes. I had cried so many times before about my mother and Jim that I didn't have many tears left.

"I'm sorry you feel that way, Rosalie. Jim loves you, he always has. He always talks about that time he found you in the parking lot skipping school. He thought you were such a beautiful little girl. But you were always a little bitch."

"I made a promise to myself years ago that that was the last time I would see Jim," I said. "Remember the nightmares I used to have? Since I made that promise, I haven't had them. I'm sorry, but there's no way I'm flying out to see him or you."

I hung up the phone before she could respond. She would never apologize or say the things a mother should say to her daughter. It just wasn't how she was. She cared more about herself than anyone else.

My body vibrated with anger and pain from the past. My chest hurt like a vice was squeezing it tight. Slowly, I walked back into the living room where David was focused on the television.

"There you are," he said. "Where's my kiss?"

He tapped his cheek, then looked at me impatiently. I gasped for air and hugged myself tightly. *He's just like my stepfather.*

"Get the fuck out of my apartment," I said.

"What?"

"You heard me. Get out. We're done. I don't want to see you ever again."

"Fucking crazy bitch," he said as he stood up.

He walked out and I slammed the door behind him. Relief rushed over me, not only for realizing how wrong David was for me, but for finally standing up for myself with my mother. It was time for me to forget the nightmares and move on.

~ *Fourteen* ~

A couple of months after breaking up with David, I found myself thinking about Shane even more. I pulled up Facebook and started scrolling through all the Shane Ventanas when I saw a photo that knocked the wind out of me. Shane was smiling in the photo with his arm around a dark-haired woman.

Bitch!

I hated her. I didn't have to know anything about her to hate her. The less I knew about her, the better. But I couldn't leave his page. I scrolled down his few public posts and then looked at his photos. He didn't seem very active on there, which was disappointing. But when I noticed the link to the name he was in a relationship with, I clicked it faster than I had ever clicked on anything before in my life.

Her name was Isabel DeLeo. *How weird that she has my last name.* She was pretty. *Bitch.* Looked similar to me with her light brown hair and dark eyes. Except she was thinner. *Double bitch.* Almost every picture of her had her looking lovingly up at Shane. *Lucky Bitch.*

From what I could tell, they were living together in Virginia. *Virginia is for lovers. Fuck you Virginia!* As I scrolled further along her page, I saw the same town name pop up over and over. It took a few minutes for it to register that the town they lived in had the same name as where I lived. That had to mean something. What were the chances that three thousand miles away, he was in the same town, just a different state?

My eyes blurred as tears filled them. I couldn't control the tears that started to fall. My chest ached. I couldn't breathe. I could still remember what his lips tasted like. How could he move on? He was supposed to be alone and miserable like me.

I was officially insane. There was no other explanation for how crazy I was acting, but I couldn't help myself. I picked up the phone and dialed Noelle. Even though we weren't as close as we were years ago, she was the only one who would understand my current insanity.

"Hello?" Noelle mumbled.

"Oh, I'm so sorry, I forgot about the time difference."

"No, it's okay, it's only the middle of the night." She laughed softly. "Everything okay?"

I sighed. "You're going to think I'm crazy."

"I already know you're crazy, nothing will change that."

"Okay, okay, but still. I need to talk and you're the only one who might understand. I'm emailing you a link."

"What is it?"

"It's Shane. I found him on Facebook."

"No shit? He still hot?"

"He looks exactly the same. His hair is a little shorter, but that's about it. Oh well, except for the woman who seems to be surgically attached to him."

"Get out! Is he married?"

"No, in a relationship. It hurts just to say that. Did you get the link?"

"Mmm-hmm. Isabel DeLeo? Is she related?"

"I know, right? That's how fucked up life is, but no relation as far as I know. Add to that, they're in the same town as me. Well, different state, but how weird is that?"

"Really weird." Noelle was quiet for a minute and I knew she was scrolling and clicking like I was. "She's pretty. Which means she's a bitch, right?"

"Yes," I said, laughing.

"You're prettier."

"You don't have to say that."

"I know, but it's true. Did you send him a friend request?"

"No, I can't.

"You okay?"

I nodded even though I knew she couldn't see me over the phone. The nod was a lie though. Even as I told myself I was okay, my throat tightened and my heart ached. Tears threatened to fall again, but I blinked them back.

"I hated how we ended things. I hated lying to him. And I hate how anytime I go on a date, I compare it to sitting in a hotel room with pints of Ben and Jerry's."

"I think that's normal. He was your first love."

"He was my only love. I still love him, Noelle."

"Then send him a friend request. Message him, something."

"No. Look at him. He's happy. I don't know how he feels about me, but I think I love him too much to cause any problems."

"You're a better person than me," she said.

"I'll be honest, it's not just that. It hurts just to see them in photos. I couldn't imagine the pain I'd feel if he actually told me he was happy or if he said he loves her. I couldn't take that."

"Then block him. Otherwise you'll keep stalking his page."

"Go back to sleep. I'll talk to you tomorrow."

"Goodnight," she said with a yawn.

I bookmarked his page.

***

As much as I tried to avoid Facebook, I found myself regularly checking if Shane posted something new and checking Isabel's page since she was more active. I was just looking at a new photo of them when my phone startled me.

"Hello?"

"Hello, Rosalie. It's your father."

"Hi, Dad. How are you?"

"I'm actually calling you about that. Promise you won't get upset, but I need to tell you something."

"Did something happen? Are you alright? You're getting me worried."

"I'm fine, but I wanted to tell you I had a stroke. The doctor called it a mini-stroke."

"Oh my God! When?"

"About a month ago."

"A month? And you're just telling me now?"

"Well, I kind of told you about it then. Remember when I told you I collapsed while I was out running?"

"You said you were okay and that it was nothing."

"I am okay. I didn't want you to worry. But Joanna said I should tell you."

"I'm coming out there," I said as I opened my laptop. "I'm going to look for the next flight. I can't believe you didn't tell me."

"No, you don't have to come, I told you everything's okay. I was in the hospital for a few days when it happened, but you know I never missed our weekly call."

I wanted to strangle my dad. He was right, he never missed our weekly call, but he never told me what really happened to him. I was grateful that he still had enough of a friendship with Joanna that she told him to tell me. But now I needed to fly out there and see for myself if he really was as okay as he said.

"There's a flight this afternoon. That'll have me in late."

"Let me know when and I'll pick you up at the airport."

"No, Dad. You are not making that drive by yourself. Call Joanna and see if she can come."

"Alright, alright. Promise you'll call me when you land."

***

The nice thing about bad news was that it provided a distraction. And the great thing about being trapped in a flying tube for six hours was that I couldn't access Facebook. I was finally able to get back to work on a book I had been working on. Unfortunately, the more I wrote, the more it turned out to be about Shane.

I needed an intervention.

It was almost midnight when the plane landed. I didn't want my father driving at that hour to pick me up, but I did promise I'd call. As the bell dinged indicating we could unfasten our seat belts, I called my dad's cell.

"Hello, Rosalie! Did you have a good flight?"

"It was good, not much turbulence. Listen, don't pick me up. It's late so I'm just going to take a cab."

"It is late, but I'm not coming to get you. Is he there yet?"

"I'm just getting off the plane now. Is who here yet?"

"Shane. Shane is coming."

Great, now I'm hearing things.

"What? I must've lost you. What did you say?"

"Shane is coming. He should be there. He's coming to pick you up."

I hung up the phone and looked at the line of people ahead of me waiting to get out of the plane.

Should I change? I look like crap. And Lord knows what my hair looks like. Why is he here?

As I got off the plane, everything began to spin. I moved out of the way and sat in the waiting area as I forced myself to breathe normally. My heart raced and for a moment I thought I was going to get sick.

What is wrong with me?

Taking a deep breath, I walked to the ladies' room and looked at myself in the mirror. I splashed some water on my face and rummaged through my bag for some lipstick to give myself some color. I pulled my hair out of the elastic holding my ponytail and ran my fingers through my hair. It wasn't perfect, but it would have to do.

I walked through the gate, pulling my bag behind me as my heart pounded. At that moment, I realized how dull my life had been since he left. Sure, I graduated college and moved across the country, but there was nothing else to my life, it was black and white.

As I stepped past security, I saw Shane standing in the middle of the walkway with an airport bouquet of flowers in his hand. He was wearing black pants and a fitted eggplant-colored shirt. His hair was brushed back with a part on the side and he had on black framed glasses which made him look even sexier, something I didn't think was possible.

A smile spread across his face when he saw me. He lifted his other hand, which held a white card with 'Princess Rosalie' neatly printed on it.

My heart leapt, reminding me what it was like to live again. As I walked faster towards him, he came to me, dropped everything, and picked me up and spun me around. I threw my arms around his neck, holding on as I laughed despite the tears that swelled in my eyes.

~ Fifteen ~

"Damn, it's so good to see you," he said.

He stopped spinning but didn't let me go. His lips suddenly pressed against mine. I sighed happily.

"Shh, don't make that sound or I might have to do you right here," he said.

Control yourself, Rosalie. Must. Not. Sigh.

He picked up the flowers and gave them to me. Then he took the handle of my bag and put his arm around my shoulders like it was the most normal thing in the world. But it wasn't normal to me. I thought things like this only happened in movies.

Does he treat his girlfriend like this? The lucky bitch.

Neither of us said anything as we left the airport. Once we got into his car, he took his glasses off and cleaned them with a cloth before he started driving.

"When did you start wearing glasses?" I asked.

"In college. All that reading did a number on my eyesight."

"You went to college?"

"Your dad didn't tell you?"

"My dad?"

"Yeah, he's really been there a lot for me. I'm surprised he didn't tell you."

"I'm realizing my dad doesn't tell me a lot of things," I said.

"He didn't tell me about the stroke either. My mother just found out the other day and told him he had to tell you. I drove up as soon as I found out."

"Oh, you drove?"

Shane clenched his jaw for a moment and a darkness spread across his face. I knew he was keeping something from me, and I suspected it was Isabel. I wanted to ask if he drove alone or if she was here too, but I was curious if he would tell me on his own.

"I've been living in Virginia for the past couple of years," he said. "After I left you, I moved to California and while I was there, I decided to go to college for Art History. I loaded up on credits and got my Bachelors in just over two years, but I didn't know what to do with it. Your dad suggested I go into teaching, so I moved to Virginia and got lucky."

"Why Virginia?"

"Because I needed to go somewhere that didn't remind me of you."

His words smacked the wind out of me. There were so many things I wanted to say, but the words wouldn't come out. I couldn't even decide if I was hurt or angry, but I kept thinking about Isabel and wondering when he was going to bring her up.

As he drove past my dad's exit, I turned to him, waiting for him to volunteer where he was taking me, but he didn't say a word.

"Where are we going?" I asked.

"To our place."

The hotel? Was he serious? After all this time he was going to act like nothing happened, like nothing changed?

"No, I'm not going there," I said. "This is ridiculous, Shane. Did you really think I'd sleep with you just because?"

"That's not why I'm taking you to the hotel."

"Yeah right. Do I look stupid? Why else would we go there?"

"Because I'm staying at my mother's and you're staying at your father's, and I think we need to talk."

"No, there's nothing to talk about. You've got a girlfriend. Were you even going to bring her up? Or did you think what happens in Jersey stays in Jersey? Because I'm telling you right now this is far from Vegas."

"You really think that's all I'm thinking about? You think I went out of my way to pick you up at the airport at midnight so I could get some pussy? Thanks a lot, Rosalie. I was never that guy, and I'm *still* not that guy."

"Then what about what you said before?"

"Maybe it was wrong, but I was only flirting. It didn't mean anything. You're right, I do have a girlfriend. Her name is Isabel and I asked her to marry me. But what fucking difference does any of that make? What about you? I'm sure you're married by now. Why don't you tell me about this amazing lucky asshole you married?"

"No! Don't say that to me. Don't talk to me like that. I...I can't even... Just take me home. Now!"

I pulled my legs up and twisted to face the window. I didn't want to be near him, let alone see him. *He asked her to marry him?!*

Do not cry. Do. Not. Cry.

I bit my lip to hold back the tears, but they fell anyway. I tried to keep my breathing calm. I couldn't control my tears, but I could keep him from knowing how much I was hurting right now. All I needed to do was face the window.

"Rosalie." His voice was soft, but it cut through me. His hand covered mine but I pulled away.

"Take me home," I choked.

~ Sixteen ~

I woke up the next morning to the smell of pancakes, my dad's specialty. After pulling my hair back into a messy ponytail, I entered the kitchen, anxious to see how my father was really doing.

"Ahh, there's my girl," he said.

I kissed my dad on the cheek as he flipped some pancakes over. He looked good, no different than the last time I saw him almost a year earlier.

Dad sat at the head of the table like he always did and I sat beside him. As he poured the syrup over his pancakes, his hand trembled slightly. If that was the worst of it, I'd take it. My dad would never tell me everything that was wrong, but at least I could see he was lucky and he really was alright.

"Is everything alright?" he asked. "You look like you have something on your mind."

"I was just worried about you, but I'm glad to see you're okay. Promise me you won't keep me in the dark about stuff like this. It's hard enough being so far from home."

"You're keeping something from me. Something else is on your mind."

I looked up from my pancakes and as I met my dad's gentle gaze, my tears from the night before came back. I didn't want to cry in front of my dad. I didn't want to cry in front of anyone. I covered my face with my hands and hoped he wouldn't ask. If I had to talk about it, I knew I'd fall apart even more.

"I know that cry," he said. He moved his chair closer to me and pulled me against his chest. "I went through that cry when your mother left me. There's nothing worse than the pain love can cause." He stroked my hair and it brought me back to when I was a child and he'd comfort me. "It's Shane, isn't it?"

I nodded as the tears came quicker. I wanted to ask my dad how he knew, but I couldn't speak. Luckily I didn't need to.

"I'm not blind," he said. "I'll admit it took me a while, but eventually I realized you two were a couple while he was living here."

"Sorry," I whispered.

"You were both adults. After he left, he would call here to speak to his mother and sometimes we'd talk. Even after Joanna and I divorced, he'd still call or visit when he was in the area. I could see how much he loved you. It's the most a father could ask for his daughter. Some people might have a problem with it since he was your stepbrother, and while he has been like a son to me, he's not my son and he never was."

My father handed me a tissue and I wiped my tears away. Somehow just hearing my father talk about Shane made me feel better. I needed to talk to Shane about last night. So much didn't make sense and I needed to set things straight.

"Rosalie, I know you. I know your mind is spinning. You're thinking and you're confused. Shane and I have spoken a lot over the past few years. And trust me, when you feel so strongly about someone like you do, you don't want to waste any time. Life is too short, honey. Talk to him."

~ Seventeen ~

I took my dad's car and drove to Joanna's apartment on the other side of town. I didn't know if Shane drove up by himself or if he'd tell me to go to hell when he saw me, but I needed to talk to him. Too much had gone unsaid for too long.

As I rang the doorbell, I heard Shane's voice from inside. I couldn't believe how nervous I felt. I tapped my foot nervously as I waited for the door to open. When he opened the door, my heart did its cartoon leap.

Shane was wearing a fitted t-shirt and jeans. His hair was messier than last night and without the glasses on, he looked just like my high school crush again.

"I didn't expect you here," he said.

"We need to talk."

"That's all I wanted from you last night."

"Fine, I'm sorry. Can I come in?"

"I don't want to talk here. I still have the room at the hotel, is that okay?"

I nodded. "Let's go."

***

The hotel looked bigger than I remembered, and it was much more crowded than it ever was on the Saturday nights Shane and I used to spend there. There was a convention at the hotel that week and the place was packed.

As we entered the elevator, a large group of tourists with their cameras squeezed in with us, forcing Shane and I to stand close together.

"If I didn't know any better, I'd think you planned this," I said.

He didn't say anything, he just smiled. His fingers brushed against my hand and I looked up at him, but he didn't look back at me. When the elevator stopped at our floor, his hand closed around mine and he pushed through the elevator to get out.

We held hands through the hall to the hotel room. Neither of us said anything, but I couldn't help but feel like my younger self five years ago when we first came here. I was excited to spend some time alone with him, even if it was just to talk. I didn't realize just how much I had missed him and how much a part of me he was until that moment.

After we entered the room, I kicked off my shoes and sat on the bed cross-legged like I used to do. He opened the mini-fridge and pulled out a pint of cookie dough Ben and Jerry's ice cream.

"I dropped it off last night before I went to the airport," he said. "I really didn't expect you to get so upset. Do you want to tell me what that was about?"

"I'm an idiot. I didn't want to hear what you were saying so I freaked."

"I need more than that." He held a spoon of ice cream up for me to eat.

"Remember what I told you the last time we were here?"

"Yes, you said you met someone. I remember that like it was yesterday. Just being here with you feels like no time has passed."

"That's exactly what happened. Seeing you at the airport, kissing you, even if it was innocent, brought me right back to where we left off. When you said you had a girlfriend--"

"You said I have a girlfriend."

"So what? You weren't going to tell me?"

"I'm not sure how relevant it is. Besides, you didn't say you were single, and you dumped me because you met someone else."

"I lied," I said. "I lied to you that night and I've regretted it every day since."

"Why would you lie about that? Do you have any idea what that did to me?"

He turned away from me and walked to the window and looked outside.

"It wasn't just you. It killed me to say that, but I thought you would be better off without me. I thought you needed to get away from here so you could make a better life for yourself. And you did. You went to school, you became a teacher--"

"And I met someone else."

His cell phone rang and he pulled it out of his pocket. For a moment, he stared at the screen with a confused expression before he answered.

"Isabel? Is everything alright?" he asked.

Does that bitch have perfect timing or what?

"No, I'm not at my mother's. I'm at the Hyatt," he said.

Shane faced me as he spoke to Isabel. Each second he was on the phone with her hurt me even more. But why was he looking at me like that? It was his old expression, the one that used to make me feel naked, but this time it was squeezing every bit of my heart and I couldn't breathe.

"Yes, that's right," he said. "I told you how I feel. It's not right. Don't make me say it again. Fine, if it'll make you feel better. I love--"

I couldn't take it anymore. I wasn't going to sit there and listen to the man I loved tell his girlfriend he loved her. I grabbed my shoes and ran out of the room and down the hall to the elevator.

As I pushed the down button, I saw Shane coming towards me. I pressed the button over and over, willing the doors to open so I could get away.

"You can't just leave like that," he said.

"Yes, I can. I just did it, didn't I? What? You think you're such hot shit that I'm going to sit there while you tell your girlfriend you love her?"

"That's not what I told her, and she is not my girlfriend."

"So now you're lying to me? I heard you."

"You're the one who lied, remember? Let's go."

He grabbed my arm and started to pull me back towards the room. I didn't have any traction in my socks so I did the only thing I could do. I threw one of my shoes at him. It hit the back of his head.

Spinning around with his mouth open with surprise, he laughed.

"You threw your shoe at me. Who throws a shoe?" he said. "That's it, you're in trouble now."

He picked me up and lifted me onto his shoulder, then kicked my shoe ahead to our room. I repeatedly hit him with my other shoe despite the fact that it did nothing. It still felt good to whack him a few times.

He dropped me on the bed and yanked my shoe out of my hand. I wasn't fighting or trying to get away, but he sat over me and held my hands down.

"Let me talk," he said. "It is not fair for you to act like this. You're acting crazy and jealous. You broke up with me, remember?"

"I know. And I know I'm acting crazy, but I can't help it. I don't know what's wrong with me."

"Then let me tell you what's wrong with me. Do you have any idea how long it took me to get over you? How long it took me to move on?"

"I don't know, but you obviously did."

"I didn't. Not a day went by that I didn't think about you. Shit, let me tell you about Isabel. Isabel is you. She has your last name, she looks similar to you, she's even a writer too. I am so fucking crazy about you that I found the next best thing, but she was never enough. She was never you."

"But you're going to marry her."

"No, I said I proposed to her, but I told you that more out of anger than anything. I was pissed I wasted so many years without you. Yes, I proposed to her, but I never said she accepted and I never said how long ago that was. She turned me down because she knew I was still in love with you. And despite how much I wanted to convince myself it wasn't true, at the airport last night, I realized she was right."

"That's bullshit!" I said angrily. "What about before on the phone?"

He sighed. "Isabel didn't take it that well. I didn't want to break up with her over the phone, but I needed to be honest with her and I didn't want to waste any more time away from you. If you hadn't come by, I was going to make damned sure you and I got to talk later."

"But I heard you! I heard you tell her you loved her on the phone."

"No, you left too soon. She wanted to hear me say again that I love *you*, Rosalie. She said it would make her feel better if she heard it again because it meant it was nothing she did." He shook his head. "I can't explain it. She didn't want to marry me, but she didn't want to break up either. I love you and I always have, ever since I first saw you as a princess."

My heart melted at his words. "I love you too."

I pulled my hands free and reached up to him as he kissed me. My heart pounded in my chest as his touch left goose bumps on my skin. It didn't matter how long it had been, my body recognized Shane's touch and demanded for more.

***

A couple days later, we went out to dinner with my dad and Shane's mother. Shane and I sat on one side of the table and my dad and Joanna sat across from us, just like that first dinner when we found out our parents got married.

Towards the end of the meal, my dad reached across the table and patted my hand.

"When are you going back to California?" he asked.

"I'm not sure," I said. "Shane has a few things to take care of in Virginia and then he's going back with me."

"That's great news!" Dad said. "What are you planning to do out there, Shane?"

"I haven't told anyone about this yet, but while I was in school I met Dmitri Nikita, my idol. We've stayed in touch over the years and he's opening a new gallery in a few months and wants to feature the series I've been working on."

"You did a series of paintings? That's incredible," I said.

"Well, they were also what led to the problems I had with Isabel. The series is about our relationship, Rosalie. You can imagine how much she hated them." He laughed. "I was never able to finish it because deep down I knew we weren't done."

"When can I see them?"

"Soon. I want you to see the series together. I've always known it needed one more painting, but nothing ever felt right. It wasn't until we got back together the other night that I knew what that last work was going to be."

Shane slipped his arm over my shoulders and pulled me closer.

"It's good to see you so happy," Joanna said.

Shane and I looked at each other and smiled.

~ Eighteen ~

Having Shane back in my life was a dream come true. We did everything together and it was like the years apart never happened.

Every day I would continue working on my book. Shane took over the spare bedroom with his art supplies. He was hard at work on the final piece of his series but refused to let me see any of them until they were displayed at the gallery.

I grew more impatient as we got closer to the gallery opening. It reached the point where I couldn't write any more because I wanted to see what he had been working on. Eager to get my mind off of it, I picked up the phone and called Noelle.

"Hey, it's Rosalie."

"Uh-oh, I recognize that voice. That's the voice you get when you need me to convince you to not do something crazy."

I laughed. "No, not this time. I just need a distraction so I figured I'd call you."

"Sure, what's going on? How are things with you and sexy Shane, your stepbrother bad boy?"

"You're just jealous."

"You're right, I am," she said with a laugh. "It seems like just yesterday you were stalking him in the halls."

"You're not helping. I'm thinking of stalking him again," I said, laughing. "I need you to get my mind off of going to the art gallery. I'm dying to see it, but Shane won't let me until everything's perfect."

"Well, you know how he is, and this is a really big deal." Noelle was quiet for a moment and then sighed. "I'm sorry, I suck as a friend because honestly, if it was me, I'd be over there already."

"Really? They crated up everything and delivered it the other day. He's been there for days now. I was thinking of surprising him."

"Go! And of course I want details."

"I'll call you tomorrow," I said as I raced out the door.

The art gallery was on the main street of Laguna Beach, just a block from the ocean. The front of the gallery was all windows and I tried to peek inside to see if I could see Shane, but all I could see were boxes and crates. As I stepped inside, the door chimed and a large man with thick grey hair, black eyes, and a sharp nose walked over to me. I knew right away he was Dmitri Nikita, artist, gallery owner, and Shane's idol.

"If you're here, you work," he said with a deep Russian accent.

"I'm here to see--"

"You see later, work first."

Seeing how he wasn't going to take no for an answer, I followed him into a windowless back room with several unopened crates. Dmitri picked up a crowbar that was leaning against the wall and brought it over to me.

"You ever use one of these?" he asked.

"No, but I'm sure I can figure it out."

"Good, I like that." He placed the crowbar under the top of one of the crates and popped it open. "Open the crates and then take each piece out. I'm sure I don't have to tell you how valuable these are."

"No, I got it."

"See me when you're done."

He started to walk out of the room, but I wasn't going to start working until I knew if Shane's pieces were there.

"Wait! Is Shane here?" I asked.

His eyes crinkled and his lips broke into a smile.

"Of course he is. And I am under strict instructions to not let you see his exhibit."

"You knew who I was?"

"Of course I know you, my dear. I've heard so much about you and I've seen his work." His face turned serious. "Now work. Work first, see later."

I unboxed all the artwork and lined them up against the wall in the back room. I had hoped to get a glimpse of something of Shane's, but Dmitri must have been expecting me because none of the paintings I unboxed belonged to Shane.

Walking out of the back room, I noticed the sun was already setting. I didn't realize how long I had been there. It must have been hours.

Shit, the meter!

I looked through my bag for quarters to feed the meter, hoping I didn't get a ticket. With a handful of change in my hand, I walked towards the front door but was stopped by Dmitri.

"You're not done," he said.

"But my car."

"It's taken care of. Come with me, Princess Rosalie."

I laughed hearing this large man, a stranger, call me that. He placed his large hand on my back and brought me to another section of the gallery. Tall white curtains stood in front of us.

"You worked, now you see," he said as he pulled the curtain back.

The space was white and lit with tiny tea light candles that formed a pathway to a circle in the middle of the room. Shane stood in the circle. A covered painting leaned against a pillar beside him. He was dressed in black pants with a dark plum button-down shirt like the day he picked me up from the airport. His sleeves were rolled up and I could see the rose tattoo on his bicep.

"How did you plan this? You didn't know I was coming here. I didn't know I was coming," I said.

"I know you better than you know yourself, Rosalie." He walked over to me, took my hand, and led me into the circle. "I knew you couldn't wait. It was just a matter of time before you showed up here."

He grinned as his arms wrapped around my waist. Spotlights lit several square paintings lined horizontally on the wall. At the end was a blank space.

"I've dreamed about today," he said. "Each of these paintings represents something in our relationship. Some people might think it's crazy, or obsessive, but even when we were apart, all I thought about was you."

He pointed to the first painting. On the canvas was a childlike princess with a young boy looking up at her. Shane lifted a handkerchief from the top of the pillar, revealing a tiara similar to the one I used to wear as a child. I laughed as he placed it on top of my head.

"You are crazy," I said.

"I'm sure you recognize the second painting, the rose. That's the one I was making for your birthday when we were living at your dad's."

"You never gave it to me."

"I never thought it was good enough."

"You should never think that. It's beautiful."

He shook his head, unable to take the compliment. I knew him well enough to not press. He would see how talented he was soon. I had no doubt that everyone would love his work.

As I looked at the different pieces, several of them really stood out to me. The first had a dark background with two white figures twisting together into one.

Another had a harsh red color and had the person from the other painting being ripped apart. He didn't need to tell me that was when we broke up, I felt his pain from the canvas. It brought all those memories back of how much I hurt him and myself. I still felt bad about that.

The last painting was swirls of colors. I felt the confusion and anger from it. My chest ached thinking about how much pain I had caused him.

"I'm sorry," I said. "I never meant to hurt you. It really was the last thing I ever wanted to do."

"Please don't be sad. It's in the past, our past, but all of my pain is there in the art. That's where it belongs.

And who knows, maybe it was meant to happen so we could be here today." He kissed my forehead and pointed to the blank space on the wall.

"Where's the final painting?"

"It's here."

He picked up the painting that was leaning against the pillar and held it up. It was similar to the harsh-colored painting but had softer colors. Instead of having two bodies in it, the painting had two hands blending together as one.

"I've been working on these for years, but I knew the series didn't end there. Now I have the ending and I'm hoping it's the beginning of our life together."

He put the painting back against the pillar and started to kneel, but the candles were in the way.

"What are you doing?" I laughed.

"I wanted to kneel for my princess, but I obviously didn't think this through all the way," he said with a smirk.

Shane reached into his pocket and pulled out a ring. He held it towards me, between his fingers, and smiled. It was a gold ring with a cluster of diamonds that formed a flower. I didn't know why the ring was familiar.

"I don't know if you recognize this ring," he said. "Before we left your dad's, I asked him for his blessing to marry you. I wanted to make sure he was alright with it."

"You mean you wanted to know if he was alright with his son marrying his daughter?" I joked.

He laughed. "Something like that. Well, he gave me this ring. He said it belonged to your grandmother."

I took the ring from him and admired it.

"I remember. She used to wear it all the time. I loved this ring."

He took the ring from me. "I'm not done."

"Well, hurry up then."

He laughed. "This isn't going how I planned. I had this whole long thing I planned on saying, but fuck it. I love you."

"I love you too."

"Will you marry me?"

"Let me think about that…umm yes."

"You had to think about it?"

"I didn't want it to be too easy," I said.

"Why not? You *are* easy, you know."

"Only with you."

"Good, that's the way it should be."

He laughed and slid the ring onto my finger. I threw myself into his arms and we kissed. I couldn't wait to begin our life together.

~ Epilogue ~

One Year Later

They say you never forget your first love. Well, Shane Ventana was my first crush, my first love, and my first heartbreak. He was my first everything, well, not *everything*, but he was the love of my life. I had never felt like I was alive until Shane entered my life. The years we were apart I felt empty without him. As sappy as it sounds, he completed me.

He was so much a part of me that I put aside the book I was working on and started a new one, a romance novel. The more I wrote, the more I wanted to tell my own story about falling in love. Eventually the book became more of a memoir than fiction, but only the people closest to me knew the truth.

The book got a lot of attention and my publisher brought Shane and me to New York for a launch party. It was surreal to me that they were making such a big deal about it that they rented a room at an upscale hotel in Midtown for the event.

Shane and I were late getting to the party. The taxi took a sharp turn, pressing me against Shane. I looked up at him and he smiled.

"I always told you you were going to be a famous writer," he said.

"It's just a party. There's no guarantee anyone is going to want to read a book about a girl falling in love with her stepbrother."

"I'd read it. And I *have* read it, it's great. You have nothing to worry about."

"You have to say that," I said.

"No, I don't. Why would I lie?"

"Because you're my husband, it's what husbands do."

He kissed my forehead as I smiled at him. He reached for my left hand and held it in his. Seeing our hands like that reminded me of the final piece of his art series.

As the taxi jolted to a stop in front of the hotel, Noelle opened the door. She held a clipboard tightly to her chest.

"It's about time," she said. "You promised you'd be here on time. You wouldn't lie to your assistant, would you?"

"Blame Shane," I said, grinning as I stepped out of the car.

"It's not my fault," he said. "You were tense so I did what I could to relax you."

"Oh, come on guys." Noelle rolled her eyes. "Can't you control yourselves for once?"

"You're just jealous," I said.

"I'm *always* jealous. Why couldn't I get a hot stepbrother?" She laughed. "But seriously, Shane, if you ever get tired of Rosalie, you know where to find me."

"I'll never get tired of her," he said as his hand slid over my butt.

"Is my dad here?" I asked.

"Of course he is," Noelle said. "You know he wouldn't miss this. He brought Joanna."

"I'm not surprised," Shane said. "They're inseparable. I never understood why they divorced."

"Me neither," I said.

The room was filled with balloons and large cardboard images of the cover. As I looked around the room for my dad, he stood up and waved at me. I walked over to where he was with Shane in tow.

"Always late," Dad said. "You know you were born late, too. That was the best day of my life." He smiled wistfully as his eyes watered. "I'm so proud of you, Rosalie."

"Thanks, Dad. It really means a lot to hear you say that."

"I've always been proud of you, you're my daughter."

I hugged him tight as tears filled my eyes. After everything that happened with my mother, I knew how lucky I was to have my dad. I blinked back my tears and sat beside him as my agent, Mena, came over.

Mena was very New York with her fancy clothes and perfect appearance. Underneath the façade, she was a fierce negotiator and one of the smartest people I knew.

"Shane," she said as she extended her hand to him. "I'm so glad to finally meet you. How do you feel about Rosalie naming the hero after you?"

"It's great. Rosalie has a great imagination." He laughed then cocked his brow at me.

"And how about you? Rosalie tells me you're an up-and-coming artist," Mena said.

"She exaggerates," he said modestly.

"I'm not exaggerating," I said. "You've been in magazines, won two awards, and there's a wait list of people demanding new pieces from you."

He shrugged. "I am working on some new things and have another exhibit in a few months. But today isn't about me, it's about Rosalie."

Shane slipped his arm around my waist and brought his lips close to my ear.

"How are you feeling? Still nauseous?" he whispered.

I shook my head, not wanting anyone to hear.

"Good. I hope you didn't mind what I told Noelle about being late."

"It's okay, I thought it was funny," I said. "Plus I'm not ready to tell everyone just yet. Not until my dad knows."

"I'm having a hard time keeping it secret."

"I know, me too. You know I can't keep secrets. I want to tell my dad in person, but not here in the middle of all of this. We can tell him and your mom tonight at dinner."

"You are going to be a wonderful mom," he said, pulling me tight against him.

"Shhh, you talk too much."

Shane kissed me and we smiled at each other. I couldn't stop smiling if I tried. We were starting a family and we couldn't be happier. I looked at the display table with my book as the centerpiece. That was my story, *our* story. Whether it was fact or fiction, I got my happily ever after.

About The Author

Veronica Daye can't imagine anything else she'd rather be doing than writing. Well except maybe reading, spending time with her family, talking about herself in the third person, or...ooh look at the butterfly!

Connect Online

www.VeronicaDaye.com

www.facebook.com/AuthorVeronicaDaye

10075474R00118

Printed in Great Britain
by Amazon.co.uk, Ltd.,
Marston Gate.